Mo

CW00972661

ᴏ ᴉ
Madness

150 years of short stories

———————————— ◆ ————————————

Edited by Frank Myszor

Series Editor: Judith Baxter

CAMBRIDGE
UNIVERSITY PRESS

PUBLISHED BY THE PRESS SYNDICATE OF THE UNIVERSITY OF CAMBRIDGE
The Pitt Building, Trumpington Street, Cambridge CB2 1RP, United Kingdom

CAMBRIDGE UNIVERSITY PRESS
The Edinburgh Building, Cambridge CB2 2RU, United Kingdom
40 West 20th Street, New York, NY 10011-4211, USA
10 Stamford Road, Oakleigh, Melbourne 3166, Australia

This edition first published 1998

Printed in the United Kingdom at the University Press, Cambridge

Typeset in Sabon 10/13 pt and Meta

A catalogue record for this book is available from the British Library

Prepared for publication by Stenton Associates

ISBN 0 521 59965 2 paperback

CONTENTS

ACKNOWLEDGEMENTS

The following copyright stories are reprinted by permission of the copyright holders, to whom grateful acknowledgement is made.

p. 9 'The Badness Within Him' by Susan Hill from *A Bit of Singing and Dancing* © Susan Hill 1971, 1972, 1973 reprinted by permission of Penguin Books; p. 19 'Day of the Butterfly' and p. 31 'Red Dress – 1946' by Alice Munro from *Dance of the Happy Shades* reprinted by permission of McGraw-Hill Ryerson Ltd; p. 45 'Killing Lizards' by William Boyd from *On the Yankee Station* reproduced by permission of the author c/o Rogers, Coleridge & White Ltd, 20 Powis Mews, London W11 1JN. Copyright © William Boyd 1981, 1982; p. 55 'Dossy' by Janet Frame from *The Lagoon and Other Stories* reproduced with permission of Curtis Brown Ltd, London on behalf of Janet Frame Clutha. Copyright © Janet Frame 1951; p. 57 'Diary of a Madman' by Nikolai Gogol from *Diary of a Madman and other stories* translated by Ronald Wilks (Penguin Classics 1972) © Ronald Wilks 1972, reproduced by permission of Penguin Books Ltd; p. 81 'The Yellow Wallpaper' by Charlotte Perkins Gilman from *The Charlotte Perkins Gilman Reader* by Ann Lane, first published in Great Britain by The Women's Press Ltd, 1981, 34 Great Sutton Street, London EC1V ODX, reprinted by permission of The Women's Press Ltd; p. 101 'Popular Mechanics' by Raymond Carver from *What We Talk About When We Talk About Love* reprinted by permission of HarperCollins Publishers Ltd; p. 103 'A Rose for Emily' by William Faulkner from *The Collected Stories of William Faulkner* reproduced by permission of Curtis Brown, London and also reprinted by permission of Random House, Inc. copyright © 1930 and renewed 1958 by William Faulkner; p. 115 'Thief' by Robley Wilson Jnr from *Dancing for Men* © 1983 reprinted by permission of the University of Pittsburgh Press; p. 119 'The July Ghost' by A.S. Byatt from *Sugar and Other Stories* reprinted by permission of the Peters Fraser & Dunlop Group Ltd; p. 137 'The Waste Land' by Alan Paton from *Debbie Go Home* reprinted with permission of Jonathan Cape and also reprinted with the permission of Scribner, a division of Simon & Schuster from *Tales from a Troubled Land* by Alan Paton. Copyright © 1961 by Alan Paton, renewed 1989 by Anne Paton; p. 141 'The Terrible Screaming' by Janet Frame from *You Are Now Entering the Human Heart* first published in Great Britain by The Women's Press Ltd, 1982, 34 Great Sutton Street, London EC1V ODX, reproduced with permission of Curtis Brown Ltd, London on behalf of Janet Frame Clutha. Copyright © Janet Frame 1983; p. 145 'Dragons' Breath' by A.S. Byatt from *The Djinn in the Nightingale's Eye* reprinted by permission of Peters Fraser & Dunlop Group Ltd.

Every effort has been made to reach copyright holders; the publishers would be glad to hear from anyone whose rights they have unknowingly infringed.

CAMBRIDGE LITERATURE

Moments of Madness is part of the Cambridge Literature series, and has been specially prepared for students in schools and colleges who are studying short stories as part of their English course.

This study edition invites you to think about what happens when you read the short stories, and it suggests that you are not passively responding to words on the page which have only one agreed interpretation, but that you are actively exploring and making new sense of what you read. Your 'reading' will partly stem from you as an individual, from your own experiences and point of view, and to this extent your interpretation will be distinctively your own. But your reading will also stem from the fact that you belong to a culture and a community, rooted in a particular time and place. So, your understanding may have much in common with that of others in your class or study group.

There is a parallel between the way you read these stories and the way they were written. The Resource Notes at the back are devised to help you to investigate the complex nature of the writing process. This begins with the author's first, tentative ideas and sources of inspiration, moves through to the stages of writing, production and publication, and ends with the text's reception by the reading public, reviewers, critics and students. So the general approach to study focuses on five key questions:

Who has written these short stories and why?

How were they produced?

What types of texts are they?

How do these short stories present their subjects?

Who reads these short stories and how do they interpret them?

These short stories are presented complete and uninterrupted. You will find some words in the text asterisked: these are words which may be unfamiliar because they have a particular cultural or linguistic significance. They are explained in the Glossary section at the back.

The Resource Notes encourage you to take an active and imaginative approach to studying these short stories both in and out of the classroom. As well as providing you with information about many aspects of them, they offer a wide choice of activities to work on individually, or in groups. Above all, they give you the chance to explore these compelling stories in a variety of ways: as a reader, an actor, a researcher, a critic, and a writer.

Judith Baxter

INTRODUCTION

A husband faints as he enters a room to find his wife on her hands and knees ... a couple hold a young baby as they argue ... a young girl refuses the gifts of another from her hospital bed – three examples of the situations created in these short stories. Some of them are literally 'moments of madness', others draw on a less extreme meaning of that expression. They refer to moments in our lives that seem to defy immediate explanation. But something has changed; from this moment things can never be the same. From the psychological crisis of growing up to the horror concealed as a woman evades paying taxes. From the terrible truth of a discovery about your own mother to the screaming that no one else can hear. What these moments have in common is that they are all in some way significant: ordinary or outlandish, these moments have been held up to be experienced and inspected. The stories in which they appear are to be read and enjoyed but also re-read and enjoyed again. Like good poetry they do not give up all of their meaning at once, so don't expect too much too soon.

Another purpose of this collection is to stand up for short stories. For too long they have existed under the shadow of the dominant form of writing in English literature – the novel – and so it is assumed that short stories and novels are read in the same way. There has also been an imbalance in the way that short stories have been presented. It is highly likely that you have been asked to write short stories but it is less likely that you have been asked (or told) how you read them. So keep in mind two important questions as you read:

- How do you read short stories compared to the way you read novels?
- What special demands do short stories make on their readers?

◆ *Pre-reading activities*

1 Before reading the stories in this collection, consider what happens when you read a novel. Think about the following and then share your views in a small group:

- your expectations about the kind of reading experience you will have (assuming it is a novel you are going to like);
- your expectations after the first page or the first chapter;
- the ingredients you are expecting;
- how you expect to feel at any point during the novel.

2 Reading novels/reading short stories

a Read the first story 'The Badness Within Him' as if it were the first chapter of a novel and record your responses as you read. If you are unsure how to do this turn to the Resource Notes on page 188. If possible, a group of readers could be given a photocopy of the story and told that it really is the first chapter of a novel.

b Then read the story again, this time as a short story, and record your responses.

c Discuss the difference that the expectation of a novel/short story can make to the same text. You might begin simply by considering length: why do you like to know how long a film is before watching it? Why do you glance at your watch to find out how long there is left? (Other readers' reactions to this task are given on page 190.)

3 Interview people about their attitudes to short stories. For example, you might try to discover who reads short stories and where they get them from.

a Brainstorm ideas for questions.

b Either as a class or in small groups, devise a questionnaire. You may need to look at examples of how this is done in magazines.

c Pool your results and in a small group present your conclusions.

For Uncle Ralph

I would also like to acknowledge the following: Jackie Baker, Lee McHugh, Vanessa Cass, Jeremy Hughes, Roger Jones, Becky Voller, William Boyd, Robley Wilson, Emma Hurst and the students of Itchen College. – FM

The Badness Within Him

Susan Hill

The night before, he had knelt beside his bed and prayed for a storm, an urgent, hysterical prayer. But even while he prayed he had known that there could he no answer, because of the badness within him, a badness which was living and growing like a cancer. So that he was not surprised to draw back the curtains and see the pale, glittering mist of another hot day. But he was angry. He did not want the sun and the endless stillness and brightness, the hard-edged shadows and the steely gleam of the sea. They came to this place every summer, they had been here, now, since the first of August, and they had one week more left. The sun had shone from the beginning. He wondered how he would bear it.

At the breakfast table, Jess sat opposite to him and her hand kept moving up to rub at the sunburned skin which was peeling off her nose.

'Stop *doing* that.'

Jess looked up slowly. This year, for the first time, Col felt the difference in age between them, he saw that Jess was changing, moving away from him to join the adults. She was almost fourteen.

'What if the skin doesn't grow again? What then? You look awful enough now.'

She did not reply, only considered him for a long time, before returning her attention to the cereal plate. After a moment, her hand went up again to the peeling skin.

Col thought, I hate it here. I hate it. I *hate* it. And he clenched his fist under cover of the table until the fingernails hurt him, digging into his palm. He had suddenly come to hate it, and the emotion frightened him. It was the reason why he had prayed for the storm, to break the pattern of long, hot, still days and waken the others out of their contentment, to change things. Now, everything was as it had always been in the past and he did not want the past, he wanted the future.

But the others were happy here, they slipped into the gentle, lazy routine of summer as their feet slipped into sandals, they never grew bored or angry or irritable, never quarrelled with one another. For days now Col had wanted to quarrel.

How had he ever been able to bear it? And he cast about, in his frustration, for some terrible event, as he felt the misery welling up inside him at the beginning of another day.

I hate it here. He hated the house itself, the chintz curtains° and covers bleached by the glare of the sun, and the crunch of sand like sugar spilled in the hall and along the tiled passages, the windows with peeling paint always open on to the garden, and the porch cluttered with sandshoes and buckets and deck-chairs, the muddle and shabbiness of it all.

They all came down to breakfast at different times, and ate slowly and talked of nothing, made no plans, for that was what the holiday was for, a respite from plans and timetables.

Fay pulled out the high chair and sat her baby down next to Col.

'You can help him with his egg.'

'Do I have to?'

Fay stared at him, shocked that anyone should not find her child desirable.

'Do help, Col, you know the baby can't manage by himself.'

'Col's got a black dog on his shoulder.'

'Shut up.'

'A perfectly enormous, coal black, monster of a dog!'

He kicked out viciously at his sister under the table. Jess began to cry.

'Now, Col, you are to apologize please.' His mother looked paler than ever, exhausted. Fay's baby dug fingers of toast down deeper and deeper into the yolk of egg.

'You hurt me, you hurt me.'

He looked out of the window. The sea was a thin, glistening line. Nothing moved. Today would be the same as yesterday and all the other days – nothing would happen, nothing would change. He felt himself itching beneath his skin.

They had first come here when he was three years old. He remembered how great the distance had seemed as he jumped from rock to rock on the beach, how he had scarcely been able to stretch his leg across and balance. Then, he had stood for minute after minute feeling the damp ribs of sand under his feet. He had been enchanted with everything. He and Jess had collected buckets full of sea creatures from the rock pools and put them into a glass aquarium in the scullery,° though always the starfish and anemones and limpets died after a few, captive days. They had taken jam jars up on to West Cliff and walked along, at the hottest part of the day, looking for chrysalis on the grass stalks. The salt had dried in white tide marks around their brown legs, and Col had reached down and rubbed some off with his finger and then licked it. In the sun lounge the moths and butterflies had swollen and cracked open their frail, papery coverings and crept out like babies from the womb, and he and Jess had sat up half the night by the light of moon or candle, watching them.

And so it had been every year and often, in winter or windy spring in London, he remembered it all, the smell of the sunlit house and the feeling of the warm sea lapping against his thighs and the line of damp woollen bathing shorts outside the open back door. It was another world, but it was still there, and when every summer came they would return to it, things would be the same.

Yet now, he wanted to do some violence in this house, he wanted an end to everything. He was afraid of himself.

'Col's got a black dog on his shoulder!'

So he left them and went for a walk on his own, over the track beside the gorse bushes and up on to the coarse grass of the sheep field behind West Cliff. The mist was rolling away, the sea was white-gold at the edges, creaming back. On the far side of the field there were poppies.

He lay down and pressed his face and hands into the warm turf until he could smell the soil beneath and, gradually, he felt the warmth of the sun on his back and it soothed him.

In the house, his mother and sisters left the breakfast table and wandered upstairs to find towels and sunhats and books, content that this day should be the same as all the other days, wanting the summer to last. And later, his father would join them for the week-end, coming down on the train from London, he would discard the blue city suit and emerge, hairy and thickly fleshed, to lie on a rug and snore and play with Fay's baby, rounding off the family circle.

By eleven it was hotter than it had been all summer, the dust rose in soft clouds when a car passed down the lane to the village, and did not settle again, and the leaves of the hedges were mottled and dark, the birds went quiet. Col felt his own anger like a pain tightening around his head. He went up to the house and lay on his bed trying to read, but the room was airless and the sunlight fell in a straight, hard beam across his bed and on to the printed page, making his eyes hurt.

When he was younger he had liked this room, he had sometimes dreamed of it when he was in London. He had collected shells and small pebbles and laid them out in careful piles, and hung up a bladder-wrack° on a nail by the open window, had brought books from home about fossils and shipwrecks and propped them on top of the painted wooden chest. But now it felt too small, it stifled him, it was a childish room, a pale, dead room in which nothing ever happened and nothing would change.

After a while he heard his father's taxi come up the drive.

'Col, do watch what you're doing near the baby, you'll get sand in his eyes.'

'Col, if you want to play this game with us, do, but otherwise go away, if you can't keep still, you're just spoiling it.'

'Col, why don't you build a sandcastle or something?'

He stood looking down at them all, at his mother and Fay playing cards in the shade of the green parasol, and his father lying on his back, his bare, black-haired chest shiny with oil and his nostrils flaring in and out as he breathed, at Jess, who had begun to build the sandcastle for the baby, instead of him. She had her hair tied back in bunches and the freckles had come out even more thickly across her cheekbones, she might have been eleven years old. But she was almost fourteen, she had gone away from him.

'Col, don't kick the sand like that, it's flying everywhere. Why don't you go and have a swim? Why can't you find something to do? I do so dislike you just hovering over us like that.'

Jess had filled a small bucket with water from the rock pool, and now she bent down and began to pour it carefully into the moat. It splashed on to her bare feet and she wriggled her toes. Fay's baby bounced up and down with interest and pleasure in the stream of water and the crenellated° golden castle.

Col kicked again more forcefully. The clods of sand hit the tower of the castle sideways, and, as it fell, crumbled the edges off the other towers and broke open the surrounding wall, so that everything toppled into the moat, clouding the water.

Jess got to her feet, scarlet in the face, ready to hit out at him.

'I hate you. *I hate you.*'

'Jess ...'

'He wants to spoil everything, look at him, he doesn't want anyone else to enjoy themselves, he just wants to sulk and ... I hate him.'

Col thought, I am filled with evil, there is no hope for me. For he felt himself completely taken over by the badness within him.

'*I hate you.*'

He turned away from his sister's wild face and her mouth which opened and shut over and over again to shout her rejection of him, turned away from them all and began to walk towards the caves at the far side of the cove. Above them were the cliffs.

Three-quarters of the way up there was a ledge around which the gannets and kittiwakes nested. He had never climbed up as high as this before. There were tussocks of grass, dried and bleached bone-pale by the sea winds, and he clung on to them and to the bumps of chalky rock. Flowers grew, pale wild scabious and cliff buttercups, and when he rested, he touched his face to them. Above his head, the sky was enamel blue. The sea birds watched him with eyes like beads. As he climbed higher, the wash of the sea and the voices of those on the beach receded. When he reached the ledge, he got his breath and then sat down cautiously, legs dangling over the edge. There was just enough room for him. The surface of the cliff was hot on his back. He was not at all afraid.

His family were like insects down on the sand, little shapes of colour dotted about at random. Jess was a pink shape, the parasol was bottle-glass green, Fay and Fay's baby were yellow. For most of the time they were still, but once they all clustered around the parasol to look at something and then broke away again, so that it was like a dance. The other people on the beach were quite separate, each family kept itself to itself. Out beyond the curve of the cliff the beach lay like a ribbon bounded by the tide, which did not reach as far as the cove except in the storms of winter. They had never been here during the winter.

When Col opened his eyes again his head swam for a moment. Everything was the same. The sky was thin and clear.

The sun shone. If he had gone to sleep he might have tipped over and fallen forwards. The thought did not frighten him.

But all was not the same, for now he saw his father had left the family group and was padding down towards the sea. The black hairs curled up the backs of his legs and the soles of his feet were brownish pink as they turned up one after the other.

Col said, do I like my father? And thought about it. And did not know.

Fay's baby was crawling after him, its lemon-coloured behind stuck up in the air.

Now, Col half-closed his eyes, so that air and sea and sand shimmered, merging together.

Now, he felt rested, no longer angry, he felt above it all.

Now, he opened his eyes again and saw his father striding into the water, until it reached up to his chest: then he flopped on to his belly and floated for a moment, before beginning to swim.

Col thought, perhaps I am ill and *that* is the badness within me.

But if he had changed, the others had changed too. Since Fay had married and had the baby and gone to live in Berkshire, she was different, she fussed more, was concerned with the details of things, she spoke to them all a trifle impatiently. And his mother was so languid. And Jess – Jess did not want his company.

Now he saw his father's dark head bobbing up and down quite a long way out to sea, but as he watched, sitting on the high cliff ledge in the sun, the bobbing stopped – began again – an arm came up and waved, though as if it were uncertain of its direction.

Col waved back.

The sun was burning the top of his head.

Fay and Fay's baby and Jess had moved in around the parasol again, their heads were bent together. Col thought, we will never be the same with one another, the ties of blood make no difference, we are separate people now. And then he felt afraid of such truth. Father's waving stopped abruptly, he bobbed and disappeared, bobbed up again.

The sea was still as glass.

Col saw that his father was drowning.

In the end, a man from the other side of the beach went running down to the water's edge and another to where the family were grouped around the parasol. Col looked at the cliff, falling away at his feet. He closed his eyes and turned around slowly and then got down on his hands and knees and began to feel for a foothold, though not daring to look. His head was hot and throbbing.

By the time he reached the bottom, they were bringing his father's body. Col stood in the shadow of the cliff and shivered and smelled the dank, cave smell behind him. His mother and Fay and Jess stood in a line, very erect, like Royalty at the cenotaph,◇ and in Fay's arms the baby was still as a doll.

Everyone else kept away, though Col could see that they made half-gestures, raised an arm or turned a head, occasionally took an uncertain step forward, before retreating again.

Eventually he wondered if they had forgotten about him. The men dripped water off their arms and shoulders as they walked and the sea ran off the body, too, in a thin, steady stream.

Nobody spoke to him about the cliff climb. People only spoke of baths and hot drinks and telephone messages, scarcely looking at one another as they did so, and the house was full of strangers moving from room to room.

In bed, he lay stiffly under the tight sheets and looked towards the window where the moon shone. He thought, it is my fault. I prayed for some terrible happening and the badness within me made it come about. I am punished. For this was a change greater than any he could have imagined.

When he slept he dreamed of drowning, and woke early, just at dawn. Outside the window, a dove grey mist muffled everything. He felt the cold linoleum under his feet and the dampness in his nostrils. When he reached the bottom of the stairs he saw at once that the door of the sun parlour was closed. He stood for a moment outside, listening to the creaking of the house, imagining all of them in their beds, his mother lying alone. He was afraid. He turned the brass doorknob and went slowly in.

There were windows on three sides of the room, long and uncurtained, with a view of the sea, but now there was only the fog pressing up against the panes, the curious stillness. The floor was polished and partly covered with rush matting and in the ruts of this the sand of all the summer past had gathered and lay, soft and gritty, the room smelled of seaweed. On the walls, the sepia photographs° of his great-grandfather the Captain, and his naval friends and their ships. He had always liked this room. When he was small, he had sat here with his mother on warm, August evenings, drinking his mug of milk, and the smell of stocks came into them from the open windows. The deck-chairs had always been in a row outside on the terrace, empty at the end of the day. He stepped forward.

They had put his father's body on the trestle, dressed in a shirt and covered with a sheet and a rug. His head was bare and lay on a cushion, and the hands, with the black hair over their backs, were folded together. Now, he was not afraid. His father's skin was oddly pale and shiny. He stared, trying to feel some sense of loss and sorrow. He had watched his father drown, though for a long time he had not believed it, the water had been so entirely calm. Later, he had heard them talking of a heart attack, and then he had understood better why this strong barrel of a man, down that day from the City, should have been so suddenly sinking, sinking.

The fog horn sounded outside. Then, he knew that the change had come, knew that the long, hot summer was at an end, and that his childhood had ended too, that they would never come to this house again. He knew, finally, the power of the badness within him and because of that, standing close to his father's body, he wept.

Day of the Butterfly

Alice Munro

I do not remember when Myra Sayla came to town, though she must have been in our class at school for two or three years. I start remembering her in the last year, when her little brother Jimmy Sayla was in Grade One.° Jimmy Sayla was not used to going to the bathroom by himself and he would have to come to the Grade Six° door and ask for Myra and she would take him downstairs. Quite often he would not get to Myra in time and there would be a big dark stain on his little button-on cotton pants. Then Myra had to come and ask the teacher: 'Please may I take my brother home, he has wet himself.'

That was what she said the first time and everybody in the front seats heard her – though Myra's voice was the lightest singsong – and there was a muted giggling which alerted the rest of the class. Our teacher, a cold gentle girl who wore glasses with thin gold rims and in the stiff solicitude° of certain poses resembled a giraffe, wrote something on a piece of paper and showed it to Myra. And Myra recited uncertainly: 'My brother has had an accident, please, teacher.'

Everybody knew of Jimmy Sayla's shame and at recess (if he was not being kept in, as he often was, for doing something he shouldn't in school) he did not dare go out on the school grounds, where the other little boys, and some bigger ones, were waiting to chase him and corner him against the back fence and thrash him with tree branches. He had to stay with Myra. But at our school there were the two sides, the Boys' Side and the Girls' Side, and it was believed that if you so much as stepped on the side that was not your own you might easily

19

get the strap. Jimmy could not go out on the Girls' Side and Myra could not go out on the Boys' Side, and no one was allowed to stay in the school unless it was raining or snowing. So Myra and Jimmy spent every recess standing in the little back porch between the two sides. Perhaps they watched the baseball games, the tag and skipping and building of leaf houses in the fall and snow forts in the winter; perhaps they did not watch at all. Whenever you happened to look at them their heads were slightly bent, their narrow bodies hunched in, quite still. They had long smooth oval faces, melancholy and discreet – dark, oily, shining hair. The little boy's was long, clipped at home, and Myra's was worn in heavy braids coiled on top of her head so that she looked, from a distance, as if she was wearing a turban too big for her. Over their dark eyes the lids were never fully raised; they had a weary look. But it was more than that. They were like children in a medieval painting, they were like small figures carved of wood, for worship or magic, with faces smooth and aged, and meekly, cryptically uncommunicative.

Most of the teachers at our school had been teaching for a long time and at recess they would disappear into the teachers' room and not bother us. But our own teacher, the young woman of the fragile gold-rimmed glasses, was apt to watch us from a window and sometimes come out, looking brisk and uncomfortable, to stop a fight among the little girls or start a running game among the big ones, who had been huddled together playing Truth or Secrets. One day she came out and called, 'Girls in Grade Six, I want to talk to you!' She smiled persuasively, earnestly, and with dreadful unease, showing fine gold rims around her teeth. She said, 'There is a girl in Grade Six called Myra Sayla. She *is* in your grade, isn't she?'

We mumbled. But there was a coo from Gladys Healey. 'Yes, Miss Darling!'

'Well, why is she never playing with the rest of you? Every day I see her standing in the back porch, never playing. Do you think she looks very happy standing back there? Do you think you would be very happy, if *you* were left back there?'

Nobody answered; we faced Miss Darling, all respectful, self-possessed, and bored with the unreality of her question. Then Gladys said, 'Myra can't come out with us, Miss Darling. Myra has to look after her little brother!'

'Oh,' said Miss Darling dubiously. 'Well you ought to try to be nicer to her anyway. Don't you think so? Don't you? You will try to be nicer, won't you? I *know* you will.' Poor Miss Darling! Her campaigns were soon confused, her persuasions turned to bleating and uncertain pleas.

When she had gone Gladys Healey said softly, 'You will try to be nicer, won't you? I *know* you will!' and then drawing her lip back over her big teeth she yelled exuberantly, 'I don't care if it rains or freezes.' She went through the whole verse and ended it with a spectacular twirl of her Royal Stuart tartan skirt. Mr. Healey ran a Dry Goods and Ladies' Wear, and his daughter's leadership in our class was partly due to her flashing plaid skirts and organdie blouses and velvet jackets with brass buttons, but also to her early-maturing bust and the fine brutal force of her personality. Now we all began to imitate Miss Darling.

We had not paid much attention to Myra before this. But now a game was developed; it started with saying, 'Let's be nice to Myra!' Then we would walk up to her in formal groups of three or four and at a signal, say together, 'Hel-lo Myra, Hello *My*-ra!' and follow up with something like, 'What do you wash your hair in, Myra, it's so nice and shiny, My-ra.' 'Oh she washes it in cod-liver oil, don't you, Myra, she washes it in cod-liver oil, can't you smell it?'

And to tell the truth there was a smell about Myra, but it was a rotten-sweetish smell as of bad fruit. That was what the Saylas did, kept a little fruit store. Her father sat all day on a stool by the window, with his shirt open over his swelling stomach and tufts of black hair showing around his belly button; he chewed garlic. But if you went into the store it was Mrs. Sayla who came to wait on you, appearing silently between the limp print curtains hung across the back of the store. Her hair was crimped in black waves and she smiled with her full lips held together, stretched as far as they would go; she told you the price in a little rapping voice, daring you to challenge her and, when you did not, handed you the bag of fruit with open mockery in her eyes.

One morning in the winter I was walking up the school hill very early; a neighbour had given me a ride into town. I lived about half a mile out of town, on a farm, and I should not have been going to the town school at all, but to a country school nearby where there were half a dozen pupils and a teacher a little demented since her change of life. But my mother, who was an ambitious woman, had prevailed on the town trustees to accept me and my father to pay the extra tuition, and I went to school in town. I was the only one in the class who carried a lunch pail and ate peanut-butter sandwiches in the high, bare, mustard-coloured cloakroom, the only one who had to wear rubber boots in the spring, when the roads were heavy with mud. I felt a little danger, on account of this; but I could not tell exactly what it was.

I saw Myra and Jimmy ahead of me on the hill; they always went to school very early – sometimes so early that they had to stand outside waiting for the janitor to open the door. They were walking slowly, and now and then Myra half turned around. I had often loitered in that way, wanting to walk with some important girl who was behind me, and not quite daring to stop and wait. Now it occurred to me that Myra might be doing this with me. I did not know what to do. I could not afford to be seen walking with her, and I did not even want to – but, on the other hand, the flattery of those humble, hopeful turnings was not lost on me. A role was shaping for me that I could not resist playing. I felt a great pleasurable rush of self-conscious benevolence; before I thought what I was doing I called, 'Myra! Hey, Myra, wait up, I got some Cracker Jack!' and I quickened my pace as she stopped.

Myra waited, but she did not look at me; she waited in the withdrawn and rigid attitude with which she always met us. Perhaps she thought I was playing a trick on her, perhaps she expected me to run past and throw an empty Cracker Jack box in her face. And I opened the box and held it out to her. She took a little. Jimmy ducked behind her coat and would not take any when I offered the box to him.

'He's shy,' I said reassuringly. 'A lot of little kids are shy like that. He'll probably grow out of it.'

'Yes,' said Myra.

'I have a brother of four,' I said. 'He's awfully shy.' He wasn't. 'Have some more Cracker Jack,' I said. 'I used to eat Cracker Jack all the time but I don't any more. I think it's bad for your complexion.'

There was a silence.

'Do you like Art?' said Myra faintly.

'No. I like Social Studies and Spelling and Health.'

'I like Art and Arithmetic.' Myra could add and multiply in her head faster than anyone else in the class.

'I wish I was as good as you. In Arithmetic,' I said, and felt magnanimous.

'But I am no good at Spelling,' said Myra. 'I make the most mistakes, I'll fail maybe.' She did not sound unhappy about this, but pleased to have such a thing to say. She kept her head turned away from me staring at the dirty snowbanks along Victoria Street, and as she talked she made a sound as if she was wetting her lips with her tongue.

'You won't fail,' I said. 'You are too good in Arithmetic. What are you going to be when you grow up?'

She looked bewildered. 'I will help my mother,' she said. 'And work in the store.'

'Well I am going to be an airplane hostess,' I said. 'But don't mention it to anybody. I haven't told many people.'

'No, I won't,' said Myra. 'Do you read Steve Canyon in the paper?'

'Yes.' It was queer to think that Myra, too, read the comics, or that she did anything at all, apart from her role at the school. 'Do you read Rip Kirby?'

'Do you read Orphan Annie?'

'Do you read Betsy and the Boys?'

'You haven't had hardly any Cracker Jack,' I said. 'Have some. Take a whole handful.'

Myra looked into the box. 'There's a prize in there,' she said. She pulled it out. It was a brooch, a little tin butterfly, painted gold with bits of coloured glass stuck onto it to look like jewels. She held it in her brown hand, smiling slightly.

I said, 'Do you like that?'

Myra said, 'I like them blue stones. Blue stones are sapphires.'

'I know. My birthstone is sapphire. What is your birthstone?'

'I don't know.'

'When is your birthday?'

'July.'

'Then yours is ruby.'

'I like sapphire better,' said Myra. 'I like yours.' She handed me the brooch.

'You keep it,' I said. 'Finders keepers.'

Myra kept holding it out, as if she did not know what I meant. 'Finders keepers,' I said.

'It was your Cracker Jack,' said Myra, scared and solemn. 'You bought it.'

'Well you found it.'

'No –' said Myra.

'Go on!' I said. 'Here, I'll *give* it to you.' I took the brooch from her and pushed it back into her hand.

We were both surprised. We looked at each other; I flushed but Myra did not. I realized the pledge as our fingers touched; I was panicky, but *all right*. I thought, I can come early and walk with her other mornings. I can go and talk to her at recess. Why not? *Why not?*

Myra put the brooch in her pocket. She said, 'I can wear it on my good dress. My good dress is blue.'

I knew it would be. Myra wore out her good dresses at school. Even in midwinter among the plaid wool skirts and serge tunics, she glimmered sadly in sky-blue taffeta,° in dusty turquoise crepe, a grown woman's dress made over, weighted by a big bow at the V of the neck and folding empty over Myra's narrow chest.

And I was glad she had not put it on. If someone asked her where she got it, and she told them, what would I say?

It was the day after this, or the week after, that Myra did not come to school. Often she was kept at home to help. But this time she did not come back. For a week, then two weeks, her desk was empty. Then we had a moving day at school and Myra's books were taken out of her desk and put on a shelf in the closet. Miss Darling said, 'We'll find a seat when she comes back.' And she stopped calling Myra's name when she took attendance.

Jimmy Sayla did not come to school either, having no one to take him to the bathroom.

In the fourth week or the fifth, that Myra had been away, Gladys Healey came to school and said, 'Do you know what – Myra Sayla is sick in the hospital.'

It was true. Gladys Healey had an aunt who was a nurse. Gladys put up her hand in the middle of Spelling and told Miss Darling. 'I thought you might like to know,' she said. 'Oh yes,' said Miss Darling. 'I do know.'

'What has she got?' we said to Gladys.

And Gladys said, 'Akemia, or something. And she has blood transfusions.' She said to Miss Darling, 'My aunt is a nurse.'

So Miss Darling had the whole class write Myra a letter, in which everybody said, 'Dear Myra, We are all writing you a letter. We hope you will soon be better and be back to school, Yours truly … .' And Miss Darling said, 'I've thought of something. Who would like to go up to the hospital and visit Myra on the twentieth of March, for a birthday party?'

I said, 'Her birthday's in July.'

'I know,' said Miss Darling. 'It's the twentieth of July. So this year she could have it on the twentieth of March, because she's sick.'

'But her *birthday* is in July.'

'Because she's sick,' said Miss Darling, with a warning shrillness. 'The cook at the hospital would make a cake and you could all give a little present, twenty-five cents or so. It would have to be between two and four, because that's visiting hours. And we couldn't all go, it'd be too many. So who wants to go and who wants to stay here and do supplementary reading?'

We all put up our hands. Miss Darling got out the spelling records and picked out the first fifteen, twelve girls and three boys. Then the three boys did not want to go so she picked out the next three girls. And I do not know when it was, but I think it was probably at this moment that the birthday party of Myra Sayla became fashionable.

Perhaps it was because Gladys Healey had an aunt who was a nurse, perhaps it was the excitement of sickness and hospitals, or simply the fact that Myra was so entirely, impressively set free of all the rules and conditions of our lives. We began to talk of her as if she were something we owned, and her party became a cause; with womanly heaviness we discussed it at recess, and decided that twenty-five cents was too low.

We all went up to the hospital on a sunny afternoon when the snow was melting, carrying our presents, and a nurse led us upstairs, single file, and down a hall past half-closed doors and dim conversations. She and Miss Darling kept saying, 'Sh-sh,' but we were going on tiptoe anyway; our hospital demeanor was perfect.

At this small country hospital there was no children's ward, and Myra was not really a child; they had put her in with two grey old women. A nurse was putting screens around them as we came in.

Myra was sitting up in bed, in a bulky stiff hospital gown. Her hair was down, the long braids falling over her shoulders and down the coverlet. But her face was the same, always the same.

She had been told something about the party, Miss Darling said, so the surprise would not upset her; but it seemed she had not believed, or had not understood what it was. She watched us as she used to watch in the school grounds when we played.

'Well, here we are!' said Miss Darling. 'Here we are!'

And we said, 'Happy birthday, Myra! Hello, Myra, happy birthday!' Myra said, 'My birthday is in July.' Her voice was lighter than ever, drifting, expressionless.

'Never mind when it is, really,' said Miss Darling. 'Pretend it's now! How old are you, Myra?'

'Eleven,' Myra said. 'In July.'

Then we all took off our coats and emerged in our party dresses, and laid our presents, in their pale flowery wrappings on Myra's bed. Some of our mothers had made immense, complicated bows of fine satin ribbon, some of them had even taped on little bouquets of imitation roses and lilies of the valley. 'Here Myra,' we said, 'here Myra, happy birthday.' Myra did not look at us, but at the ribbons, pink and blue and speckled with silver, and the miniature bouquets; they pleased her, as the butterfly had done. An innocent look came into her face, a partial, private smile.

'Open them, Myra,' said Miss Darling. 'They're for you!'

Myra gathered the presents around her, fingering them, with this smile, and a cautious realization, an unexpected pride. She said, 'Saturday I'm going to London to St. Joseph's Hospital.'

'That's where my mother was at,' somebody said. 'We went and saw her. They've got all nuns there.'

'My father's sister is a nun,' said Myra calmly.

She began to unwrap the presents, with an air that not even Gladys could have bettered, folding the tissue paper and the ribbons, and drawing out books and puzzles and cutouts as if they were all prizes she had won. Miss Darling said that maybe she should say thank you, and the person's name with every gift she opened, to make sure she knew whom it was from, and so Myra said, 'Thank you, Mary Louise, thank you, Carol,' and when she came to mine she said, 'Thank you, Helen.' Everyone explained their presents to her and there was talking and excitement and a little gaiety, which Myra presided over, though she was not gay. A cake was brought in with *Happy Birthday Myra* written on it, pink on white, and eleven candles. Miss Darling lit the candles and we all sang Happy Birthday to You, and cried, 'Make a wish, Myra, make a wish –' and Myra blew them out. Then we all had cake and strawberry ice cream.

At four o'clock a buzzer sounded and the nurse took out what was left of the cake, and the dirty dishes, and we put on our coats to go home. Everybody said, 'Goodbye, Myra,' and Myra sat in the bed watching us go, her back straight, not supported by any pillow, her hands resting on the gifts. But at the door I heard her call; she called, 'Helen!' Only a couple of the others heard; Miss Darling did not hear, she had gone out ahead. I went back to the bed.

Myra said, 'I got too many things. You take something.'

'What?' I said. 'It's for your birthday. You always get a lot at a birthday.'

'Well you take something,' Myra said. She picked up a leatherette case with a mirror in it, a comb and a nail file and a natural lipstick and a small handkerchief edged with gold thread. I had noticed it before. 'You take that,' she said.

'Don't you want it?'

'You take it.' She put it into my hand. Our fingers touched again.

'When I come back from London,' Myra said, 'you can come and play at my place after school.'

'Okay,' I said. Outside the hospital window there was a clear carrying sound of somebody playing in the street, maybe chasing with the last snowballs of the year. This sound made Myra, her triumph and her bounty, and most of all her future in which she had found this place for me, turn shadowy, turn dark. All the presents on the bed, the folded paper and ribbons, those guilt-tinged offerings, had passed into this shadow, they were no longer innocent objects to be touched, exchanged, accepted without danger. I didn't want to take the case now but I could not think how to get out of it, what lie to tell. I'll give it away, I thought, I won't ever play with it. I would let my little brother pull it apart.

The nurse came back, carrying a glass of chocolate milk.

'What's the matter, didn't you hear the buzzer?'

So I was released, set free by the barriers which now closed about Myra, her unknown, exalted, ether-smelling° hospital world, and by the treachery of my own heart. 'Well thank you,' I said. 'Thank you for the thing. Goodbye.'

Did Myra ever say goodbye? Not likely. She sat in her high bed, her delicate brown neck rising out of a hospital gown too big for her, her brown carved face immune to treachery, her offering perhaps already forgotten, prepared to be set apart for legendary uses, as she was even in the back porch at school.

Red Dress – 1946

Alice Munro

My mother was making me a dress. All through the month of November I would come from school and find her in the kitchen, surrounded by cut-up red velvet and scraps of tissue-paper pattern. She worked at an old treadle machine° pushed up against the window to get the light, and also to let her look out, past the stubble fields and bare vegetable garden, to see who went by on the road. There was seldom anybody to see.

The red velvet material was hard to work with, it pulled, and the style my mother had chosen was not easy either. She was not really a good sewer. She liked to make things; that is different. Whenever she could she tried to skip basting° and pressing and she took no pride in the fine points of tailoring, the finishing of buttonholes and the overcasting of seams as, for instance, my aunt and my grandmother did. Unlike them she started off with an inspiration, a brave and dazzling idea; from that moment on, her pleasure ran downhill. In the first place she could never find a pattern to suit her. It was no wonder; there were no patterns made to match the ideas that blossomed in her head. She had made me, at various times when I was younger, a flowered organdie° dress with a high Victorian neckline edged in scratchy lace, with a poke bonnet° to match; a Scottish plaid outfit with a velvet jacket and tam;° an embroidered peasant blouse worn with a full red skirt and black laced bodice. I had worn these clothes with docility, even pleasure, in the days when I was unaware of the world's opinion. Now, grown wiser, I wished for dresses like those my friend Lonnie had, bought at Beale's store.

I had to try it on. Sometimes Lonnie came home from school with me and she would sit on the couch watching. I was embarrassed by the way my mother crept around me, her knees creaking, her breath coming heavily. She muttered to herself. Around the house she wore no corset or stockings, she wore wedge-heeled shoes and ankle socks; her legs were marked with lumps of blue-green veins. I thought her squatting position shameless, even obscene; I tried to keep talking to Lonnie so that her attention would be taken away from my mother as much as possible. Lonnie wore the composed, polite, appreciative expression that was her disguise in the presence of grownups. She laughed at them and was a ferocious mimic, and they never knew.

My mother pulled me about, and pricked me with pins. She made me turn around, she made me walk away, she made me stand still. 'What do you think of it, Lonnie?' she said around the pins in her mouth.

'It's beautiful,' said Lonnie, in her mild, sincere way. Lonnie's own mother was dead. She lived with her father who never noticed her, and this, in my eyes, made her seem both vulnerable and privileged.

'It *will* be, if I can ever manage the fit,' my mother said. 'Ah, well,' she said theatrically, getting to her feet with a woeful creaking and sighing, 'I doubt if she appreciates it.' She enraged me, talking like this to Lonnie, as if Lonnie were grown up and I were still a child. 'Stand still,' she said, hauling the pinned and basted dress over my head. My head was muffled in velvet, my body exposed, in an old cotton school slip. I felt like a great raw lump, clumsy and goose-pimpled. I wished I was like Lonnie, light-boned, pale and thin; she had been a Blue Baby.°

'Well nobody ever made me a dress when I was going to high school,' my mother said, 'I made my own, or I did without.' I was afraid she was going to start again on the story

32

of her walking seven miles to town and finding a job waiting on tables in a boarding-house, so that she could go to high school. All the stories of my mother's life which had once interested me had begun to seem melodramatic, irrelevant, and tiresome.

'One time I had a dress given to me,' she said. 'It was a cream-coloured cashmere wool* with royal blue piping down the front and lovely mother-of-pearl* buttons, I wonder what ever became of it?'

When we got free Lonnie and I went upstairs to my room. It was cold, but we stayed there. We talked about the boys in our class, going up and down the rows and saying, 'Do you like him? Well, do you half-like him? Do you *hate* him? Would you go out with him if he asked you?' Nobody had asked us. We were thirteen, and we had been going to high school for two months. We did questionnaires in magazines, to find out whether we had personality and whether we would be popular. We read articles on how to make up our faces to accentuate our good points and how to carry on a conversation on the first date and what to do when a boy tried to go too far. Also we read articles on frigidity of the menopause, abortion and why husbands seek satisfaction away from home. When we were not doing school work, we were occupied most of the time with the garnering, passing on and discussing of sexual information. We had made a pact to tell each other everything. But one thing I did not tell was about this dance, the high school Christmas Dance for which my mother was making me a dress. It was that I did not want to go.

At high school I was never comfortable for a minute. I did not know about Lonnie. Before an exam, she got icy hands and palpitations, but I was close to despair at all times. When I was asked a question in class, any simple little question at all, my voice was apt to come out squeaky, or else hoarse and trembling. When I had to go to the blackboard I was sure –

even at a time of the month when this could not be true – that I had blood on my skirt. My hands became slippery with sweat when they were required to work the blackboard compass. I could not hit the ball in volleyball; being called upon to perform an action in front of others made all my reflexes come undone. I hated Business Practice because you had to rule pages for an account book, using a straight pen, and when the teacher looked over my shoulder all the delicate lines wobbled and ran together. I hated Science; we perched on stools under harsh lights behind tables of unfamiliar, fragile equipment, and were taught by the principal of the school, a man with a cold, self-relishing voice – he read the Scriptures every morning – and a great talent for inflicting humiliation. I hated English because the boys played bingo at the back of the room while the teacher, a stout, gentle girl, slightly cross-eyed, read Wordsworth at the front. She threatened them, she begged them, her face red and her voice as unreliable as mine. They offered burlesqued° apologies and when she started to read again they took up rapt postures, made swooning faces, crossed their eyes, flung their hands over their hearts. Sometimes she would burst into tears, there was no help for it, she had to run out into the hall. Then the boys made loud mooing noises; our hungry laughter – oh, mine too – pursued her. There was a carnival atmosphere of brutality in the room at such times, scaring weak and suspect people like me.

But what was really going on in the school was not Business Practice and Science and English, there was something else that gave life its urgency and brightness. That old building, with its rock-walled clammy basements and black cloakrooms and pictures of dead royalties and lost explorers, was full of the tension and excitement of sexual competition, and in this, in spite of daydreams of vast successes, I had premonitions of total defeat. Something had to happen, to keep me from that dance.

With December came snow, and I had an idea. Formerly I had considered falling off my bicycle and spraining my ankle and I had tried to manage this, as I rode home along the hard-frozen, deeply rutted country roads. But it was too difficult. However, my throat and bronchial tubes were supposed to be weak; why not expose them? I started getting out of bed at night and opening my window a little. I knelt down and let the wind, sometimes stinging with snow, rush in around my bared throat. I took off my pajama top. I said to myself the words 'blue with cold' and as I knelt there, my eyes shut, I pictured my chest and throat turning blue, the cold, greyed blue of veins under the skin. I stayed until I could not stand it any more, and then I took a handful of snow from the windowsill and smeared it all over my chest, before I buttoned my pajamas. It would melt against the flannelette° and I would be sleeping in wet clothes, which was supposed to be the worst thing of all. In the morning, the moment I woke up, I cleared my throat, testing for soreness, coughed experimentally, hopefully, touched my forehead to see if I had fever. It was no good. Every morning, including the day of the dance, I rose defeated, and in perfect health.

The day of the dance I did my hair up in steel curlers. I had never done this before, because my hair was naturally curly, but today I wanted the protection of all possible female rituals. I lay on the couch in the kitchen, reading *The Last Days of Pompeii*,° and wishing I was there. My mother, never satisfied, was sewing a white lace collar on the dress; she had decided it was too grown-up looking. I watched the hours. It was one of the shortest days of the year. Above the couch, on the wallpaper, were old games of Xs and Os,° old drawings and scribblings my brother and I had done when we were sick with bronchitis. I looked at them and longed to be back safe behind the boundaries of childhood.

When I took out the curlers my hair, both naturally and artificially stimulated, sprang out in an exuberant glossy bush.

I wet it, I combed it, beat it with the brush and tugged it down along my cheeks. I applied face powder, which stood out chalkily on my hot face. My mother got out her Ashes of Roses Cologne, which she never used, and let me splash it over my arms. Then she zipped up the dress and turned me around to the mirror. The dress was princess style, very tight in the midriff. I saw how my breasts, in their new stiff brassiere, jutted out surprisingly, with mature authority, under the childish frills of the collar.

'Well I wish I could take a picture,' my mother said. 'I am really, genuinely proud of that fit. And you might say thank you for it.'

'Thank you,' I said.

The first thing Lonnie said when I opened the door to her was, 'Jesus, what did you do to your hair?'

'I did it up.'

'You look like a Zulu. Oh, don't worry. Get me a comb and I'll do the front in a roll. It'll look all right. It'll even make you look older.'

I sat in front of the mirror and Lonnie stood behind me, fixing my hair. My mother seemed unable to leave us. I wished she would. She watched the roll take shape and said, 'You're a wonder, Lonnie. You should take up hairdressing.'

'That's a thought,' Lonnie said. She had on a pale blue crepe dress, with a peplum° and bow; it was much more grown-up than mine even without the collar. Her hair had come out as sleek as the girl's on the bobby-pin° card. I had always thought secretly that Lonnie could not be pretty because she had crooked teeth, but now I saw that crooked teeth or not, her stylish dress and smooth hair made me look a little like a golliwog, stuffed into red velvet, wide-eyed, wild-haired, with a suggestion of delirium.

My mother followed us to the door and called out into the dark, 'Au reservoir!' This was a traditional farewell of Lonnie's and mine; it sounded foolish and desolate coming from her,

36

and I was so angry with her for using it that I did not reply. It was only Lonnie who called back cheerfully, encouragingly, 'Good night!'

The gymnasium smelled of pine and cedar. Red and green bells of fluted paper° hung from the basketball hoops; the high, barred windows were hidden by green boughs. Everybody in the upper grades seemed to have come in couples. Some of the Grade Twelve and Thirteen girls had brought boy friends who had already graduated, who were young businessmen around the town. These young men smoked in the gymnasium, nobody could stop them, they were free. The girls stood beside them, resting their hands casually on male sleeves, their faces bored, aloof and beautiful. I longed to be like that. They behaved as if only they – the older ones – were really at the dance, as if the rest of us, whom they moved among and peered around, were, if not invisible, inanimate; when the first dance was announced – a Paul Jones – they moved out languidly, smiling at each other as if they had been asked to take part in some half-forgotten childish game. Holding hands and shivering, crowding up together, Lonnie and I and the other Grade Nine girls followed.

I didn't dare look at the outer circle as it passed me, for fear I should see some unmannerly hurrying-up. When the music stopped I stayed where I was, and half-raising my eyes I saw a boy named Mason Williams coming reluctantly towards me. Barely touching my waist and my fingers, he began to dance with me. My legs were hollow, my arm trembled from the shoulder, I could not have spoken. This Mason Williams was one of the heroes of the school; he played basketball and hockey and walked the halls with an air of royal sullenness and barbaric contempt. To have to dance with a nonentity like me was as offensive to him as having to memorize Shakespeare. I felt this as keenly as he did, and imagined that he was exchanging looks of dismay with his friends. He steered me,

37

stumbling, to the edge of the floor. He took his hand from my waist and dropped my arm.

'See you,' he said. He walked away.

It took me a minute or two to realize what had happened and that he was not coming back. I went and stood by the wall alone. The Physical Education teacher, dancing past energetically in the arms of a Grade Ten boy, gave me an inquisitive look. She was the only teacher in the school who made use of the words social adjustment, and I was afraid that if she had seen, or if she found out, she might make some horribly public attempt to make Mason finish out the dance with me. I myself was not angry or surprised at Mason; I accepted his position, and mine, in the world of school and I saw that what he had done was the realistic thing to do. He was a Natural Hero, not a Student Council type of hero bound for success beyond the school; one of those would have danced with me courteously and patronizingly and left me feeling no better off. Still, I hoped not many people had seen. I hated people seeing. I began to bite the skin on my thumb.

When the music stopped I joined the surge of girls to the end of the gymnasium. Pretend it didn't happen, I said to myself. Pretend this is the beginning, now.

The band began to play again. There was movement in the dense crowd at our end of the floor, it thinned rapidly. Boys came over, girls went out to dance. Lonnie went. The girl on the other side of me went. Nobody asked me. I remembered a magazine article Lonnie and I had read, which said *Be gay! Let the boys see your eyes sparkle, let them hear laughter in your voice! Simple, obvious, but how many girls forget!* It was true, I had forgotten. My eyebrows were drawn together with tension, I must look scared and ugly. I took a deep breath and tried to loosen my face. I smiled. But I felt absurd, smiling at no one. And I observed that girls on the dance floor, popular girls, were not smiling; many of them had sleepy, sulky faces and never smiled at all.

Girls were still going out to the floor. Some, despairing, went with each other. But most went with boys. Fat girls, girls with pimples, a poor girl who didn't own a good dress and had to wear a skirt and sweater to the dance; they were claimed, they danced away. Why take them and not me? Why everybody else and not me? I have a red velvet dress, I did my hair in curlers, I used a deodorant and put on cologne. *Pray*, I thought. I couldn't close my eyes but I said over and over again in my mind, *Please, me, please,* and I locked my fingers behind my back in a sign more potent than crossing, the same secret sign Lonnie and I used not to be sent to the blackboard in Math.

It did not work. What I had been afraid of was true. I was going to be left. There was something mysterious the matter with me, something that could not be put right like bad breath or overlooked like pimples, and everybody knew it, and I knew it; I had known it all along. But I had not known it for sure, I had hoped to be mistaken. Certainty rose inside me like sickness. I hurried past one or two girls who were also left and went into the girls' washroom. I hid myself in a cubicle.

That was where I stayed. Between dances girls came in and went out quickly. There were plenty of cubicles; nobody noticed that I was not a temporary occupant. During the dances, I listened to the music which I liked but had no part of any more. For I was not going to try any more. I only wanted to hide in here, get out without seeing anybody, get home.

One time after the music started somebody stayed behind. She was taking a long time running the water, washing her hands, combing her hair. She was going to think it funny that I stayed in so long. I had better go out and wash my hands, and maybe while I was washing them she would leave.

It was Mary Fortune. I knew her by name, because she was an officer of the Girls' Athletic Society and she was on the Honour Roll and she was always organizing things. She had something to do with organizing this dance; she had been around to all the classrooms asking for volunteers to do the decorations. She was in Grade Eleven or Twelve.

'Nice and cool in here,' she said. 'I came in to get cooled off. I get so hot.'

She was still combing her hair when I finished my hands. 'Do you like the band?' she said.

'It's all right.' I didn't really know what to say. I was surprised at her, an older girl, taking this time to talk to me.

'I don't. I can't stand it. I hate dancing when I don't like the band. Listen. They're so choppy. I'd just as soon not dance as dance to that.'

I combed my hair. She leaned against a basin, watching me.

'I don't want to dance and don't particularly want to stay in here. Let's go and have a cigarette.'

'Where?'

'Come on, I'll show you.'

At the end of the washroom there was a door. It was unlocked and led into a dark closet full of mops and pails. She had me hold the door open, to get the washroom light, until she found the knob of another door. This door opened into darkness.

'I can't turn on the light or somebody might see,' she said. 'It's the janitor's room.' I reflected that athletes always seemed to know more than the rest of us about the school as a building; they knew where things were kept and they were always coming out of unauthorized doors with a bold, preoccupied air. 'Watch out where you're going,' she said. 'Over at the far end there's some stairs. They go up to a closet on the second floor. The door's locked at the top, but there's like a partition between the stairs and the room. So if we sit on the steps, even if by chance someone did come in here, they wouldn't see us.'

'Wouldn't they smell smoke?' I said.

'Oh, well. Live dangerously.'

There was a high window over the stairs which gave us a little light. Mary Fortune had cigarettes and matches in her purse. I had not smoked before except the cigarettes Lonnie and I made ourselves, using papers and tobacco stolen from her father; they came apart in the middle. These were much better.

'The only reason I even came to-night,' Mary Fortune said, 'is because I am responsible for the decorations and I wanted to see, you know, how it looked once people got in there and everything. Otherwise why bother? I'm not boy-crazy.'

In the light from the high window I could see her narrow, scornful face, her dark skin pitted with acne, her teeth pushed together at the front, making her look adult and commanding.

'Most girls are. Haven't you noticed that? The greatest collection of boy-crazy girls you could imagine is right here in this school.'

I was grateful for her attention, her company and her cigarette. I said I thought so too.

'Like this afternoon. This afternoon I was trying to get them to hang the bells and junk. They just get up on the ladders and fool around with boys. They don't care if it ever gets decorated. It's just an excuse. That's the only aim they have in life, fooling around with boys. As far as I'm concerned, they're idiots.'

We talked about teachers, and things at school. She said she wanted to be a Physical Education teacher and she would have to go to college for that, but her parents did not have enough money. She said she planned to work her own way through, she wanted to be independent anyway, she would work in the cafeteria and in the summer she would do farm work, like picking tobacco. Listening to her, I felt the acute phase of my unhappiness passing. Here was someone who had suffered the same defeat as I had – I saw that – but she was full of energy and self respect. She had thought of other things to do. She would pick tobacco.

We stayed there talking and smoking during the long pause in the music, when, outside, they were having doughnuts and coffee. When the music started again Mary said, 'Look, do we

41

have to hang around here any longer? Let's get our coats and go. We can go down to Lee's and have a hot chocolate and talk in comfort, why not?'

We felt our way across the janitor's room, carrying ashes and cigarette butts in our hands. In the closet, we stopped and listened to make sure there was nobody in the washroom. We came back into the light and threw the ashes into the toilet. We had to go out and cut across the dance-floor to the cloakroom, which was beside the outside door.

A dance was just beginning. 'Go round the edge of the floor,' Mary said. 'Nobody'll notice us.'

I followed her. I didn't look at anybody. I didn't look for Lonnie. Lonnie was probably not going to be my friend any more, not as much as before anyway. She was what Mary would call boy-crazy.

I found that I was not so frightened, now that I had made up my mind to leave the dance behind. I was not waiting for anybody to choose me. I had my own plans. I did not have to smile or make signs for luck. It did not matter to me. I was on my way to have a hot chocolate, with my friend.

A boy said something to me. He was in my way. I thought he must be telling me that I had dropped something or that I couldn't go that way or that the cloakroom was locked. I didn't understand that he was asking me to dance until he said it over again. It was Raymond Bolting from our class, whom I had never talked to in my life. He thought I meant yes. He put his hand on my waist and almost without meaning to, I began to dance.

We moved to the middle of the floor. I was dancing. My legs had forgotten to tremble and my hands to sweat. I was dancing with a boy who had asked me. Nobody told him to, he didn't have to, he just asked me. Was it possible, could I believe it, was there nothing the matter with me after all?

I thought that I ought to tell him there was a mistake, that I was just leaving, I was going to have a hot chocolate with my girl friend. But I did not say anything. My face was making certain delicate adjustments, achieving with no effort at all the grave absent-minded look of those who were chosen, those who danced. This was the face that Mary Fortune saw, when she looked out of the cloakroom door, her scarf already around her head. I made a weak waving motion with the hand that lay on the boy's shoulder, indicating that I apologized, that I didn't know what had happened and also that it was no use waiting for me. Then I turned my head away, and when I looked again she was gone.

Raymond Bolting took me home and Harold Simons took Lonnie home. We all walked together as far as Lonnie's corner. The boys were having an argument about a hockey game, which Lonnie and I could not follow. Then we separated into couples and Raymond continued with me the conversation he had been having with Harold. He did not seem to notice that he was now talking to me instead. Once or twice I said, 'Well I don't know I didn't see that game,' but after a while I decided just to say 'H'm hmm,' and that seemed to be all that was necessary.

One other thing he said was, 'I didn't realize you lived such a long ways out.' And he sniffled. The cold was making my nose run a little too, and I worked my fingers through the candy wrappers in my coat pocket until I found a shabby Kleenex. I didn't know whether I ought to offer it to him or not, but he sniffled so loudly that I finally said, 'I just have this one Kleenex, it probably isn't even clean, it probably has ink on it. But if I was to tear it in half we'd each have something.'

'Thanks,' he said. 'I sure could use it.'

It was a good thing, I thought, that I had done that, for at my gate, when I said, 'Well, good night,' and after he said, 'Oh, yeah. Good night,' he leaned towards me and kissed me, briefly, with the air of one who knew his job when he saw it, on the corner of my mouth. Then he turned back to town, never knowing he had been my rescuer, that he had brought me from Mary Fortune's territory into the ordinary world.

I went around the house to the back door, thinking, I have been to a dance and a boy has walked me home and kissed me. It was all true. My life was possible. I went past the kitchen window and I saw my mother. She was sitting with her feet on the open oven door, drinking tea out of a cup without a saucer. She was just sitting and waiting for me to come home and tell her everything that had happened. And I would not do it, I never would. But when I saw the waiting kitchen, and my mother in her faded, fuzzy Paisley kimono,° with her sleepy but doggedly expectant face, I understood what a mysterious and oppressive obligation I had, to be happy, and how I had almost failed it, and would be likely to fail it, every time, and she would not know.

Killing Lizards

William Boyd

Gavin squatted beside Israel, the cook's teenage son, on the narrow verandah of the servants' quarters. Israel was making Gavin a new catapult. He bound the thick, rubber thongs to the wooden Y with string, tying the final knot tight and nipping off the loose ends with his teeth. Gavin took the proffered catapult and tried a practice shot. He fired at a small grove of banana trees by the kitchen garden. The pebble thunked into a fibrous bole° with reassuring force.

'Great!' Gavin said admiringly, then 'hey!' as Israel snatched the catapult back. He dangled the weapon alluringly out of Gavin's reach and grinned as the small twelve-year-old boy leapt angrily for it.

'Cig'rette. Give me cig'rette,' Israel demanded, laughing in his high wheezy way.

'Oh, all right,' Gavin grudgingly replied, handing over the packet he had stolen from his mother's handbag the day before. Israel promptly lit one up and confidently puffed smoke up into the washed out blue of the African sky.

Gavin walked back up the garden to the house. He was a thin dark boy with a slightly pinched face and unusually thick eyebrows that made his face seem older than it was. He went through the kitchen and into the cool spacious living room with its rugs and tiled floor, where two roof fans energetically beat the hot afternoon air into motion.

The room was empty and Gavin walked along the verandah past his bedroom and that of his older sister. His sister, Amanda, was at boarding school in England; Gavin was going

45

to join her there next year. He used to like his sister but since her fifteenth birthday she had changed. When she had come out on holiday last Christmas she had hardly played with him at all. She was bored with him; she preferred going shopping with her mother. A conspiracy of sorts seemed to have sprung up between the women of the family from which Gavin and his father were excluded.

When he thought of his sister now, he felt that he hated her. Sometimes he wished the plane that was bringing her out to Africa would crash and she would be killed. Then there would only be Gavin, he would be the only child. As he passed her bedroom he was reminded of his fantasy and despite himself he paused, thinking about it again, trying to imagine what life would be like – how it would be different. As he did so the other dream began to edge itself into his mind, like an insistent hand signalling at the back of a classroom drawing attention to itself. He had this dream quite a lot these days and it made him feel peculiar: he knew it was bad, a wrong thing to do, and sometimes he forced himself not to think about it. But it never worked, for it always came faltering back with its strange imaginative allure, and he would find himself lost in it, savouring its pleasures, indulging in its sweet illicit sensations.

It was a variation on the theme of his sister's death, but this time it also included his father. His father and sister had died in a car crash and Gavin had to break the news to his mother. As she sobbed with grief she clung to him for support. Gavin would soothe her, stroking her hair as he'd seen done on TV in England, whispering words of comfort.

In the dream Gavin's mother never remarried, and she and Gavin returned to England to live. People would look at them in the street, the tall elegant widow in black and her son, growing tall and more mature himself, being brave and good by her side. People around them seemed to whisper, 'I don't know what she would have done without him' and 'Yes, he's been a marvel' and 'They're so close now'.

Gavin shook his head, blushing guiltily. He didn't hate his father – he just got angry with him sometimes – and it made him feel bad and upset that he kept on imagining him dead. But the dream insistently repeated itself, and it continued to expand; the narrative furnished itself with more and more precise details; the funeral scene was added, the cottage Gavin and his mother took near Canterbury, the plans they made for the school holidays. It grew steadily more real and credible – it was like discovering a new world – but as it did, so Gavin found himself more and more frustrated and oppressed by the truth, more dissatisfied with the way things were.

Gavin slowly pushed open the door of his parents' bedroom. Sometimes he knocked, but his mother had laughed and told him not to be silly. Still, he was cautious as he had once been horribly embarrassed to find them both asleep, naked and sprawled on the rumpled double bed. But today he knew his father was at work in his chemistry lab. Only his mother would be having a siesta.

But Gavin's mother was sitting in front of her dressing table brushing her short but thick reddish auburn hair. She was wearing only a black bra and pants that contrasted strongly with the pale freckly tan of her firm body. A cigarette burned in an ashtray. She brushed methodically and absentmindedly, her shining hair crackling under the brush. She seemed quite unaware of Gavin standing behind her, looking on. Then he coughed.

'Yes, darling, what is it?' she said without looking round.

Gavin sensed rather than appreciated that his mother was a beautiful woman. He did not realize that she was prevented from achieving it fully by a sulky turn to her lips and a hardness in her pale eyes. She stood up and stretched languidly, walking bare-footed over to the wardrobe where she selected a cotton dress.

'Where are you going?' Gavin asked without thinking.

'Rehearsal, dear. For the play,' his mother replied.

'Oh. Well, I'm going out too.' He left it at that. Just to see if she'd say anything this time, but she seemed not to have heard. So he added, 'I'm going with Laurence and David. To kill lizards.'

'Yes, darling,' his mother said, intently examining the dress she had chosen. 'Do try not to touch the lizards, they're nasty things, there's a good boy.' She held the dress up in front of her and looked at her reflection critically in the mirror. She laid the dress on the bed, sat down again and began to apply some lipstick. Gavin looked at her rich red hair and the curve of her spine in her creamy back, broken by the dark strap of her bra, and the three moles on the curve of her haunch where it was tautened by the elastic of her pants. Gavin swallowed. His mother's presence in his life loomed like a huge wall at whose foot his needs cowered like beggars at a city gate. He wished she bothered about him more, did things with him as she did with Amanda. He felt strange and uneasy about her, proud and uncomfortable. He had been pleased last Saturday when she took him to the pool in town, but then she had worn a small bikini and the Syrian men round the bar had stared at her. David's mother always wore a swimsuit of a prickly material with stiff bones in it. When he went out of the room she was brushing her hair again and he didn't bother to say good-bye.

Gavin walked down the road. He was wearing a striped T-shirt, white shorts and Clarks sandals without socks. The early afternoon sun beat down on his head and the heat vibrated up from the tarmac. On either side of him were the low senior-staff bungalows, shadowy beneath their wide eaves, and which seemed to be pressed down into the earth as if the blazing sun bore down with intolerable weight. The coruscating* scarlet dazzle of flamboyant trees that lined the road danced spottily in his eyes.

The university campus was a large one but Gavin had come to know it intimately in the two years since his parents had moved to Africa. In Canterbury his father had only been a lecturer but here he was a professor in the Chemistry Department. Gavin loved to go down to the labs with their curious ammoniacal° smells, brilliant fluids and mad-scientist constructions of phials,° test-tubes and rubber pipes. He thought he might pay his father a surprise visit that afternoon as their lizard hunt should take them in that direction.

Gavin and his two friends had been shooting lizards with their catapults for the three weeks of the Easter holidays and had so far accounted for one hundred and forty-three. They killed mainly the male and female of one species that seemed to populate every group of boulders or area of concrete in the country. The lizards were large, sometimes growing to eighteen inches in length. The females were slightly smaller than the males and were a dirty speckled khaki colour. The males were more resplendent, with brilliant orange-red heads, pale grey bodies and black-barred feet and tails. They did no one any harm; just basked in the sun doing a curious bobbing press-up motion. At first they were ludicrously easy to kill. The boys could creep up to within three or four feet and with one well-placed stone reduce the basking complacent lizard to a writhing knot, its feet clawing at a buckled spine or shattered head. A slight guilt had soon grown up among the boys and they accordingly convinced themselves that the lizards were pests and that, rather like rats, they spread diseases.

But the lizards, like any threatened species, grew wise to the hunters and now scurried off at the merest hint of approach, and the boys had to range wider and wider through the campus to find zones where the word had not spread and where the lizards still clung unconcernedly to walls, like dozing sun-bathers unaware of the looming thunderclouds.

Gavin met his friends at the pre-arranged corner. Today they were heading for the university staff's preparatory school at a far edge of the campus. There was an expansive outcrop of boulders there with a sizeable lizard community that they had been evaluating for some time, and this afternoon they planned a blitz.

They walked down the road firing stones at trees and clumps of bushes. Gavin teased Laurence about his bandy legs and then joined forces with him to mock David about his spots and his hugely fat sister until he threatened to go home. Gavin felt tense and malicious, and lied easily to them about how he had fashioned his own catapult, which was far superior to their clumsier home-made efforts. He was glad when they rounded a corner and came in sight of the long simple buildings of the chemistry labs.

'Let's go and see my Dad,' he suggested.

Gavin's father was marking exam papers in an empty lab when the three boys arrived. He was tall and thin with sparse black hair brushed across his balding head. Gavin possessed his similar tentative smile. They chatted for a while, then Gavin's father showed them some frozen nitrogen. He picked a red hibiscus bloom off a hedge outside and dipped it in the container of fuming liquid. Then he dropped the flower on the floor and it shattered to pieces like fine china.

'Where are you off to?' he asked as the boys made ready to leave.

'Down to the school to get lizards,' Gavin replied.

'There's a monster one down there,' said David. 'I've seen it.'

'I hope you don't leave them lying around,' Gavin's father said. 'Things rot in this sun very quickly.'

'It's okay,' Gavin affirmed brightly. 'The hawks soon get them.'

Gavin's father looked thoughtful. 'What's your mother doing?' he asked his son. 'Left her on her own, have you?'

'Israel's there,' Gavin replied sullenly. 'But anyway she's going to her play rehearsal or something. Drama, drama, you know.'

'Today? Are you sure?' his father asked, seemingly surprised.

'That's what she said. Bye, Dad, see you tonight.'

The school lay on a small plateau overlooking a teak forest and the jungle that stretched away beyond it. The outcrop of rocks was poised on the edge of the plateau and it ran down in pale pinkish slabs to the beginning of the teak trees.

The boys killed four female lizards almost at once but the others had rushed into crevices and stayed there. Gavin caught a glimpse of a large red-head as it scuttled off and the three of them pelted the deep niche it hid in and prodded at it with sticks, but it was just not coming out.

Then Gavin and Laurence thought they saw a fruit bat in a palm tree, but David couldn't see it and soon lost interest. They patrolled the deserted school buildings for a while and then hung, bat-like themselves, on the Jungle-Jim° in the playground. David, who had perched on the top, heard the sound of a car as it negotiated a bumpy rutted track that led into the jungle and which ran for a while along the base of the plateau. He soon saw a Volkswagen van lurching along. A man was driving and a woman sat beside him.

'Hey, Gavin,' David said without thinking. 'Isn't that your mother?'

Gavin climbed quickly up beside him and looked.

'No,' he said. 'Nope. Definitely.'

They resumed their play but the implication hung in the air like a threat, despite their suddenly earnest jocularity. In the unspoken way in which these things arrange themselves, David and Laurence soon announced that they had to go home. Gavin said that he would stay on a bit. He wanted to see if he could get that big lizard.

Laurence and David wandered off with many a backward shouted message about where they would meet tomorrow and what they would do. Then Gavin clambered about half-heartedly on the Jungle-Jim before he walked down the slope to the track which he followed into the teak forest. There was still heat in the afternoon sun and the trees and bushes looked tired from a day's exposure. The big soup-plate leaves of the teak trees hung limply in the damp dusty atmosphere.

Gavin heard his mother's laugh before he saw the van. He moved off the track and followed the curve of a bend until he saw the van through the leaves. It was pulled up on the other side of the mud road. The large sliding door was thrown back and Gavin could see that the bunk bed inside had been folded down. His mother was sitting on the edge of the bunk, laughing. A man without a shirt was struggling to zip up her dress. She laughed again, showing her teeth and throwing back her head, joyously shaking her thick red hair. Gavin knew the man: he was called Ian Swan and sometimes came to the house. He had a neat black beard and curling black hair all over his chest.

Gavin stood motionless behind the thick screen of leaves and watched his mother and the man. He knew at once what they had been doing. He watched them caper and kiss and laugh. Finally Gavin's mother tugged herself free and scrambled round the van and into the front seat. Gavin saw a pair of sunglasses drop from her open handbag. She didn't notice they had fallen. Swan put on his shirt and joined her in the front of the van.

As they backed and turned the van Gavin held his breath in an agony of tension in case they should run over the glasses. When they had gone he stood for a while before walking over and picking up the sunglasses. They were quite cheap; Gavin remembered she had bought them last leave in England. They were favourites. They had pale blue lenses and candy-pink frames. He held them carefully in the palm of his hand as if he were holding an injured bird.

MUMMY ...

As he walked down the track to the school the numbness, the blank camera stare that had descended on him the moment he had heard his mother's high laugh, began to dissipate. A slow tingling charge of triumph and elation began to infuse his body.

OH, MUMMY, I THINK …

He looked again at the sunglasses in his palm. Things would change now. Nothing would be the same after this secret. It seemed to him now as if he were carrying a ticking bomb.

OH, MUMMY, I THINK I'VE FOUND YOUR SUNGLASSES.

The lowering sun was striking the flat rocks of the outcrop full on and Gavin could feel the heat through the soles of his sandals as he walked up the slope. Then, ahead, facing away from him, he saw the lizard. It was catching the last warmth of the day, red head methodically bobbing, sleek torso and long tail motionless. Carefully Gavin set down the glasses and took his catapult and a pebble from his pocket. Stupid lizard, he thought, sunbathing, head bobbing like that, you never know who's around. He drew a bead on it, cautiously easing the thick rubber back to full stretch until his rigid left arm began to quiver from the tension.

He imagined the stone breaking the lizard's back, a pink welling tear in the pale scaly skin. The curious slow-motion way the mortally wounded creatures keeled over, sometimes a single leg twitching crazily like a spinning rear wheel on an upended crashed car.

The lizard basked on, unaware.

Gavin eased off the tension. Holding his breath with the effort, heart thumping in his ears. He stood for a few seconds letting himself calm down. His mother would be home now, he should have enough time before his father returned. He picked up the sunglasses and backed softly away and around leaving the lizard undisturbed. Then, with his eyes alight and gleaming beneath his oddly heavy brows, he set off steadily for home.

Dossy

Janet Frame

Only on the shadows, sang out Dossy, and the little girls with straight fair hair sang out answering, only on the shadows, and the two of them went hopping and skipping very carefully for three blocks, and then they got tired, and they forgot, and they stopped to pick marigolds through the crack in the corner fence, but only Dossy could reach them because she was bigger.

– Pick me a marigold, Dossy, to put in my hair, said the little girl, and Dossy picked a big yellow flower and she had to bend down to stick it in the little girl's hair.

– Race you to the convent gate, she said, and together the two of them tore along the footpath and Dossy won, Dossy won easily.

– I'm bigger, she said.

And the little girl looked up at Dossy's bigness and supposed that Dossy must live in a big house to match. Everything matched, thought the little girl. Mother and Father. Mother singing and Father singing. Mother washing the dishes and Father drying. Mother in her blue dress and Father in his black suit.

And when you were small you did things that small people did, Grandma said, and when you were big like Dossy you did things the grown-up way. And the little girl thought that Dossy must live in a big house to match her bigness. A big house at the end of a long long street. With a garden. And a plum tree. And a piano in the front room. And a piano-stool to go round and round on. And lollies in a blue tin on the mantelpiece for

Father to reach up to and say, have a striped one, chicken, they last longer.

The little girl put her hand in Dossy's and said, can I come to live with you, Dossy? Can I live in your house?

And Dossy looked down at the little girl with her shiny new shoes on and her neat blue dress and her thick hair-ribbon, and then she looked down at her own dirty shoes and turned-up dress from her aunties, and she drew away her hand that was dirty and sticky with marigolds and said nothing, but went over to the fence to peep through at the nuns. The little girl followed her and together they looked through at the nuns. They watched them walking up and down with their hands folded in front and their eyes staring straight ahead, and the little girl thought, I'll be a nun some day and wear black and white and have a black and white nightie, and I'll pray all day and sit under the plum tree and perhaps God won't mind if I get hungry and eat two or three plums, and every night I'll comb out my mother's long golden hair with a gold comb and I'll have a black and white bed.

– Dossy, said the little girl, will you be a nun with me?

Dossy giggled and giggled. I don't think, she said.

The nuns heard someone laughing and they stopped at the gate to see who it was. They saw a little girl playing ball by herself on the footpath.

– It's little Dossy Park, they said. With no mother and living in that poky little house in Hart Street and playing by herself all the time, goodness knows what she'll turn out to be.

Diary of a Madman

Nikolai Gogol

October 3rd

Something very peculiar happened today. I got up rather late, and when Mavra brought my clean shoes in I asked her what the time was. When she told me it was long past ten I rushed to get dressed. To be honest with you, if I'd known the sour look I was going to get from the head of our department I wouldn't have gone to the office at all. For some time now he's been saying: 'Why are you always in such a muddle? Sometimes you rush around like a madman and make such a mess of your work, the devil himself couldn't sort it out. You start paragraphs with small letters and leave out the date and reference number altogether.' Damned old buzzard! Seeing me in the Director's° office sharpening His Excellency's° quills must have made him jealous. To cut a long story short, I'd never have gone to the office in the first place if there hadn't been a good chance of seeing the cashier and making the old Jew cough up a small advance somehow or other. What a man! The Last Judgement will be upon us before you can get a month's pay out of *him* in advance. Even if you're down to your last kopeck,° you can go on asking until you're blue in the face, but that old devil won't give in. I've heard people say his own cook slaps him on the face in the flat. The whole world knows about it. I don't see there's any advantage working in our department. No perks at all. It's a different story in the Provincial Administration or in the Civil or Treasury Offices. You'll see someone sitting there curled up in a corner scribbling away. He'll be wearing a filthy old frock coat and just one look at his mug is enough to make you spit. But you should see the country house he rents! Just offer him a gilt china cup and all he'll say is: 'That's what you give a *doctor*!' He'll only be satisfied with a pair of racehorses, or a drozhky,◇ or a beaver skin that cost three hundred roubles.◇ To look at him you'd think he was so meek and mild, and he talks with such refinement: 'Please be so good as to lend me that little knife to sharpen my quills.' But just give him the chance and he'll strip any petitioner◇ until there's only the shirt left on his back. I must admit, it's very civilized working in our department, everything's kept cleaner than you'll ever see in a Provincial Office. And we have mahogany tables, and all the Principals◇ use the polite form of address. But really, if it weren't for the snob value, I'd have given in my notice long ago.

I put on my old overcoat and took my umbrella, as it was simply teeming down outside. There wasn't a soul about; all I could see were a few old peasant women sheltering under their skirts, some Russian merchants under their umbrellas and one or two messengers. As for better-class people, there weren't any, except for a civil servant.◇ I spotted him at the crossroads. As soon as I saw him I said to myself: 'Aha, you're not going to the office, my friend, you're after that girl dashing along over there – and having a good look at her legs into the bargain.' What beasts our civil servants are! Good God, they'd leave any officer standing and get their claws into anything that goes past in a bonnet. While I was engrossed with these thoughts, a carriage drew up in front of a shop I happened to be passing. I saw at once this was our Director's. He couldn't be wanting anything in there, so he must have called for his daughter, I thought. I flattened myself against the wall. A footman opened the carriage door and out she fluttered, just like a little bird. The way she looked first to the right, then to the left, her eyes and her eyebrows flashing past ... God in heaven, I thought, I'm lost, lost forever! Strange *she* should venture out in all that rain! Now just you try and tell me women aren't mad on clothes. She didn't recognize me, and I tried to muffle myself up as best I could, because my overcoat, besides being covered all over in stains, had gone out of fashion ages ago. Nowadays they're all wearing coats with long collars, but mine were short, one over the other. And you couldn't really say the cloth had been waterproofed.

Her little dog wasn't quite quick enough to nip in after her and had to stay out in the street. I'd seen that dog before. She's called Medji. I hadn't been there more than a minute when I heard a faint little voice: 'Hello, Medji!' Well, I never! Who was that talking? I looked around and saw two ladies walking along under an umbrella: one was old, but her companion was quite young. They'd already gone past when I heard that voice again: 'Shame on you, Medji!' What was going on, for heaven's sake? Then I saw Medji sniffing round a little dog following the two ladies. 'Aha,' I said to myself, 'it can't be true, I must be drunk.' But I hardly ever drink. 'No Fidèle,' I told myself, 'you're quite mistaken.' With my own eyes I actually saw Medji mouth these words: 'I've been, bow wow, very ill, bow wow.' Ah, you nasty little dog! I must confess I was staggered to hear it speak just like a human being. But afterwards, when I'd time to think about it, my amazement wore off. In fact, several similar cases have already been reported. It's said that in England a fish swam to the surface and said two words in such a strange language the professors have been racking their brains for three years now to discover what it was, so far without success. What's more, I read somewhere in the papers about two cows going into a shop to ask for a pound of tea. Honestly, I was much more startled when I heard Medji say: 'I *did* write to you, Fidèle. Polkan couldn't have delivered my letter.' I'd stake a month's salary that that was what the dog said. Never in my life have I heard of a dog that could write. Only noblemen know how to write correctly. Of course, you'll always find some traders or shopkeepers, even serfs, who can scribble away: but they write like machines – no commas or full stops, and simply no idea of style.

I was really astonished at all this. To be frank, quite recently I've started hearing and seeing things I'd never heard or seen before. So I said to myself, 'I'd better follow this dog and find out who she is and what she's thinking about.' I unrolled my umbrella and followed the two ladies. We crossed Gorokhovaya Street, turned into Meshchanskaya Street, then Stolyanaya Street, until we got to Kokushkin Bridge and stopped in front of a large house. 'I know this house,' I said to myself; 'it's Zverkov's.' What a dump! Everybody seems to live there: crowds of cooks, foreigners, civil servants. They live just like dogs, all on top of each other. A friend of mine who plays the trumpet very well lives there. The ladies went up to the fifth floor. 'Fine,' I thought. 'I shan't go in now, but I'll make a note of the address and come back as soon as I have a moment to spare.'

October 4th

Today is Wednesday, and that's why I went to see the head of our department in his office. I made sure I got there early and sat down to sharpen all the quills.

Our Director must be a very clever man: his study is full of shelves crammed with books. I read some of their titles: such erudition, such scholarship! Quite above the head of any ordinary civil servant. All in French or German. And you should look into his face, and see the deep seriousness that gleams in his eyes! I have yet to hear him use *one* more word than is necessary. He might perhaps ask as you handed him some papers: 'What's the weather like?' And you would reply, 'Damp today, Your Excellency.' No, you can't compare him with your ordinary clerk. He's a true statesman. May I say, however, that he has a special fondness for me. If only his daughter ... scum that I am! Never mind, better say nothing about that. I've been reading the *Little Bee*.◊ A crazy lot, those French! What *do* they want? My God, I'd like to give them all

a good flogging. There was a very good account of a ball
written by a landowner from Kursk.° They certainly know how
to write, those landowners from Kursk! At that moment I
noticed it was already past 12.30 and that our Director hadn't
left his bedroom. But about 2.30 something happened that no
pen could adequately describe. The door opened. I thought it
was the Director and leapt up from my chair, clutching my
papers: but it was her, herself in person! Holy Fathers, how she
was dressed! Her dress was white, like a swan. What
magnificence! And when she looked at me it was like the sun
shining, I swear it! She nodded and said: 'Has papa been here?'
Oh what a voice! A canary, just like a canary! I felt like saying
to her: 'Your Excellency, don't have me put to death, but if
that is your wish, then let it be by your own noble hand.' But
I was almost struck dumb, blast it, and all I could mumble was
'No, Miss.' She looked at me, then at the books, and dropped
her handkerchief. I threw myself at it, slipped on the damned
parquet floor and nearly broke my nose. I regained my balance
however, and picked up the handkerchief. Heavens, what a
handkerchief! Such a fine lawn, and smelling just like pure
ambergris.°

You could tell from the smell it belonged to a general's
daughter. She thanked me, and came so near to smiling that
her sweet lips almost parted, and with that she left. I worked
on for about another hour until a footman suddenly appeared
with the message: 'You can go home now, Axenty Ivanovich,
the master's already left the house.' I can't stand that brood of
flunkeys: they're always sprawled out in the hall and it's as
much as you can do to get one little nod of acknowledgement
from them. What's more, one of those pigs once offered me
some snuff – without even getting up. Don't you know,
ignorant peasant, that I am a civil servant and of noble birth?
All the same, I picked up my hat, put my coat on *myself* –
because those fine gentlemen wouldn't dream of helping you –

and left the office. For a long time I lay on my bed at home. Then I copied out some very fine poetry:

> An hour without seeing you
> Is like a whole year gone by
> How wretched my life's become
> Without you I'll only fret and sigh.

Must be something by Pushkin.° In the evening I wrapped myself up in my overcoat and went to Her Excellency's house, and waited a long time outside the entrance just to see her get into her carriage once more. But no, she didn't come out.

November 6th

The head of the department was in a terrible mood. When I got to the office he called me in and took this line with me: 'Will you please tell me what your game is.' 'Why, nothing,' I answered. 'Are you sure? Think hard! You're past forty now, and it's time you had a bit more sense. Who do you think you are? Do you imagine I haven't heard about your tricks? I know you've been running after the Director's daughter! Take a good look at yourself. *What* are you? Just nothing, an absolute *nobody*. You haven't a kopeck to bless yourself with. Just take a look in the mirror – fancy *you* having thoughts about the General's° daughter!' To hell with it, his own face puts you in mind of those large bottles you see in chemists' windows, what with that tuft of hair he puts in curlers. And the way he holds his head up and smothers his hair in pomade!° Thinks he can get away with anything! Now I can understand why he's got it in for me: seeing me get some preferential treatment in the office has made him jealous. I don't care a hoot about him! Just because he's a court councillor he thinks he's Lord God Almighty! He lets his gold watch chain dangle outside his waistcoat and pays thirty roubles for a pair of shoes. He can go to hell! Does he think I'm the son of a commoner, or tailor, or a non-commissioned officer? I'm a gentleman! I could get promotion if I wanted! I'm only forty-two, that's an age nowadays when one's career is only just beginning. Just you wait, my friend, until I'm a colonel, or even something higher, God willing. I'll get more respect than *you*. Where did you get the idea *you're* the only person whom we're supposed to look up to around here? Just give me a coat from Ruch's,° cut in the latest style; I'll knot my tie like you do: and then you won't be fit to clean my boots. It's only that I'm short of money.

November 8th

I went to the theatre today. The play was about the Russian fool, Filatka.° I couldn't stop laughing. They also put on some sort of vaudeville with some amusing little satirical poems about lawyers, and one Collegiate Registrar° in particular. So near the knuckle, I wonder they got past the censor. As for merchants, the author says straight out that they're swindling everyone and that their sons lead a dissolute life and have thoughts of becoming members of the aristocracy. There was a very witty couplet about the critics, saying they do nothing but pull everything to pieces, so the author asks for the audience's protection. A lot of very amusing plays are being written these days. I love going to the theatre. As long as I've a kopeck in my pocket you can't stop me. But these civil servants of ours are such ignorant pigs, you'd never catch *those* peasants going, even if you gave them a ticket for nothing. One of the actresses sang very well. She reminded me of … ah! I'm a shocker! … Silence! The less said the better!

November 9th

At eight o'clock I set off for the office. The head of the department pretended he hadn't seen me come in. I played the same game, just as if we were complete strangers. Then I started checking and sorting out some documents. At four o'clock I left. I passed the Director's flat, but there didn't seem to be anybody in. After dinner I lay on my bed most of the evening.

November 11th

Today I sat in the Director's office and sharpened twenty-three quills for him – and for *her*. Ah, four quills for Her Excellency! He loves having a lot of pens around the place. Really, he must have a very fine brain! He doesn't say very much, but you can sense his mind is working the whole time. I'd like to know what he's hatching in that head of his. And those people with all their puns and court jokes – I wish I knew more about them and what goes on at that level of society.

Often I've thought of having a good talk with His Excellency, but somehow I'm always stuck for words: I begin by saying it's cold or warm outside, and that's as far as I get. I'd like to have a peep into the drawing-room but all I ever manage to see is another door which is sometimes open, and leads off to another room. Ah, what luxury! The china and mirrors! I'd love to see that part of the house where Her Excellency ... yes, that's what I'd dearly love to see, her boudoir, with all those jars and little phials, and such flowers, you daren't even breathe on them. To see her dress lying there, more like air than a dress. And just one peep in her bedroom to see what wonders lie there, sheer paradise, more blissful than heaven. One glance at that little stool where she puts her tiny foot when she steps out of bed. And then, over that tiny foot, she starts pulling on her snowy white stocking. Ah, never mind, never mind, enough said ...

Today something suddenly dawned on me which made everything clear: I recalled the conversation I'd heard between the two dogs on Nevsky Avenue. I thought to myself 'Good, now I'll find out what it's all about. Somehow I must get hold of the letters that passed between those two filthy little dogs. There's sure to be something there.' To be frank, once I very nearly called Medji and said: 'Listen, Medji, we're alone now.

If you want I'll shut the door so no one can see. Tell me everything you know about the young lady, who she is and what she's like. I swear I won't tell a soul.'

But that crafty dog put her tail between her legs, seemed to shrink to half her size, and went quietly out through the door, as though she had heard nothing. I'd suspected for a long time that dogs are cleverer than human beings. I was even convinced she could speak if she wanted to, but didn't, merely out of sheer cussedness. Dogs are extraordinarily shrewd, and notice everything, every step you take. No, whatever happens, I shall go to the Zverkovs' tomorrow and cross-examine Fidèle, and with any luck I'll get my hands on all the letters Medji wrote to her.

November 12th

At two in the afternoon I set off with the firm intention of seeing Fidèle and cross-examining her. I can't stand the smell of cabbage; the shops along the Meshchanskaya just reek of it. What with this, and the infernal stench coming from under the front doors of all the houses, I held my nose and ran for all I was worth.

If that's not bad enough, those beastly tradesmen let so much soot and smoke pour out of their workshops that it's quite impossible for any respectable gentleman to take a stroll these days.

When I reached the sixth floor and rang the bell, a quite pretty-looking girl with tiny freckles came to the door. I recognized her as the same girl I'd seen walking with the old lady. She blushed slightly and straight away I realized that the little dear needed a boyfriend. 'What do you want?' she said. 'I must have a talk with your dog,' I replied. The girl was quite stupid – I could see that at once. While I was standing there the dog came out barking at me. I tried to catch hold of her but the nasty little bitch nearly sank her teeth into my nose. However, I spotted her basket in the corner. That's what I was after! I went over to it, rummaged around under the straw and to my great delight pulled out a small bundle of papers. Seeing this, that filthy dog first bit me on the thigh and then, when she'd sniffed around and discovered I'd taken the papers, started whining and pawing me, but I said to her: 'No, my dear, good-bye!' and took to my heels. The girl must have thought I was mad, as she seemed scared out of her wits.

When I arrived home, I intended starting work right away sorting the papers out, because I can't see all that well by candlelight. But Mavra decided the floor needed washing. Those stupid Finns always take it into their heads to have a good clean up at the most inconvenient times. So I decided to go for a walk and have a good think about what had happened earlier. Now at last I would find out every little detail of what had been going on, what was in their minds, who were the main actors in the drama, in fact, nothing would be hidden from me: those letters would tell me everything. 'Dogs are a clever species,' I told myself. 'They're well versed in diplomacy, and therefore everything will be written down, including a description of the Director and his private life. And there'll be something about *her*, but never mind that now … Silence!' I returned home towards the evening and spent most of the time lying on my bed.

November 13th

Well now, let's have a look: the letter is quite legible, though the handwriting looks a bit doggy. Let's see: 'Dear Fidèle, I still can't get used to your plebeian° name. Couldn't they find a better one for you? Fidèle, like Rosa, is in very vulgar taste. However, all that's neither here nor there. I am very glad we decided to write to each other.'

The letter is impeccably written. The punctuation is correct and even the letter 'ye'° is in the right place. Even the head of our department can't put a letter together so well, for all his telling us that he went to some university or other. Let's see what else there is: 'I think that sharing thoughts, feelings and experiences with another person is one of the greatest blessings in this life.' Hm! He must have found that in some translation from the German. The name escapes me for the moment.

'I am speaking from experience, though I've never ventured further than our front door. Don't you think I lead a very agreeable life? My mistress, whom Papa calls Sophie, is passionately fond of me.'

Ah! Never mind! Silence!

'Papa often likes to fondle and stroke me as well. I take cream with my tea and coffee. Ah, *ma chère*! I really must tell you, I don't get any pleasure out of those large half-gnawed bones our Polkan likes guzzling in the kitchen. I only like bones from game-birds, and then only if the marrow hasn't already been sucked out by someone else. A mixture of several different sauces can be very tasty, as long as you don't put any capers or greens in. But in my opinion there's nothing worse than little pellets of dough. There's usually some gentleman sitting at the table who starts kneading bread with hands that not long before have been in contact with all sorts of filth. He'll call you over and stick a pellet between your teeth. It's rather bad manners to refuse, and you have to eat it though it's quite disgusting ...'

What on earth does all that mean? Never read such rubbish! As if they didn't have anything better to write about! Let's look at another page and see if we can find something with a bit more sense in it.

'I should be delighted to tell you about everything that goes on in our house. I've already mentioned something about the head of the house, whom Sophie calls Papa. He's a very strange man.'

Ah, at last! Yes, I knew it all the time: their approach is very diplomatic. Let's see what they say about this Papa.

'... a very strange man. Says nothing most of the time. He speaks very rarely; but a week ago he kept on saying to himself: "Will I get it, will I get it?" Once he turned to me and asked, "What do you think, Medji? Will I get it, or won't I?" I couldn't understand a word he was saying. I sniffed his shoes and left the room. Then, *ma chère*, about a week later he came home beaming all over. The whole morning men in uniforms kept arriving to congratulate him on something or other. During dinner Papa was gayer than ever I'd seen him before, telling anecdotes and afterwards lifting me up to his shoulders and saying: "Look, Medji, what's that?" It was some sort of ribbon. I sniffed at it, but it didn't have any sort of smell at all. Then I gave it a furtive lick, and it tasted rather salty.'

Hm! That dog, in my opinion, is going too far ... She'll be lucky if she doesn't get a whipping! Ah, he's so ambitious! Must make a note of that.

'Good-bye, *ma chère*. I'm in a tearing hurry, etc. etc. ... I'll finish the letter tomorrow. Well, hello, here I am again. Today my mistress Sophie ...'

Aha! Let's see what she says about Sophie. Ah, you devil! Never mind, never mind ... Let's get on with it.

' ... my mistress Sophie was in such a tizzy. She was getting dressed for a ball, and I was delighted to have the chance of writing to you while she was gone. My Sophie is always thrilled to go to a ball, although getting ready usually puts her in a bad temper. I really can't understand, *ma chère*, what pleasure there is in going to these balls. Sophie comes home about six in the morning, and I can always tell from the poor dear's pale, thin look that she's had nothing to eat. I must confess *that* would be no life for me. If I didn't have woodcock done in sauce or roast chicken wings I don't know what would become of me ... Sauce goes very well with gruel. But you can't do anything with carrots or turnips, or artichokes ...'

The style is amazingly jerky. You can see at once that it's not written by a human being. It starts off all right, and then lapses into dogginess ... Let's have a look at another letter. Seems rather long. Hm, there's no date either!

'Ah, my dear, how deeply I feel the approach of spring! My heart is beating as though it were waiting for something.

There's a perpetual noise in my ears, and I often raise a paw and stand listening at the door for several minutes. In confidence, I must tell you I have a great many suitors. I often sit watching them out of the window. Ah, if you only knew how ugly some of them are! There's one very coarse mongrel, so stupid you can see it written all over his face, and he swaggers down the street thinking he's someone very important and that everyone else thinks the same. But he's wrong. I ignored him completely, just as if I'd never set eyes on him. And that terrifying Great Dane that keeps stopping by my window! If he stood on his hind legs (the coarse clodhopper's not even capable of that) he'd be a whole head taller than Sophie's Papa – and as you know, *he's* tall enough – and plump into the bargain. The great lump has the cheek of the devil. I growled at him, but a fat lot he cared. He just frowned back, stuck his tongue out, dangled his enormous ears and kept staring straight at the window – the peasant! But don't imagine, *ma chère*, that my heart is indifferent to all these suitors, ah, no … If you'd seen one gallant called Trésor, who climbed over the fence from next door. Ah my dear, you should see his little muzzle!'

Ugh, to hell with it! What trash! Fancy filling a letter with such nonsense! I need *people*, not dogs! I want to see a human being; I ask for spiritual nourishment to feed and delight my soul, but all I end up with is that rubbish! Let's skip a page and see if there's something better.

'Sophie was sitting at a small table and sewing. I was looking out of the window as I love to see who's going by. All of a sudden a footman came into the room and said: "Teplov." "Ask him in," cried Sophie and threw her arms around me. "Ah, Medji, Medji, if you could only see him: a Guards Officer with brown hair, and his eyes – what eyes! – black, and shining bright as fire!"'

'Sophie ran up to her room. A minute later in came a young gentleman with black whiskers. He went up to the mirror, smoothed his hair and looked round the room. I snarled and settled down by the window. Soon Sophie appeared and gaily curtseyed as he clicked his heels. I kept looking out of the window just as if they weren't there, but I tried to catch what they were saying by cocking my head to one side. Ah, *ma chère*! What rubbish they talked! About a certain lady who danced the wrong step at a ball, and someone called Bobov who looked just like a stork in his jabot,° and who nearly fell over. And there was someone called Lidina who thought she had blue eyes, whereas they were really green, and so on. How can one compare, I asked myself, this gentleman of the court with Trésor? Good heavens, they're whole worlds apart! First of all, the young gentleman's face is wide and very smooth and has whiskers growing all round it, just as if someone had bound it up with a black handkerchief. But Trésor's muzzle is very thin, and he has a white spot on his forehead. And you can't compare their figures. And Trésor's eyes, his bearing, aren't the same at all. What a difference! I really don't know what she can see in this court chamberlain. Why is she so crazy about him?'

It strikes me something's not quite right here. How can a young court chamberlain sweep her off her feet like that? Let's have a look:

'I think that if she can care for that court chamberlain then she can easily feel the same for the civil servant who has a desk in Papa's study. Ah, *ma chère*, if only you knew how ugly he is! Just like a tortoise in a sack.'

What is this civil servant like?

'He has a very peculiar name. All the time he sits sharpening quills. His hair looks just like hay. Papa always sends him on errands instead of one of the servants.'

I think that nasty little dog is referring to me. Who says my hair is like hay?

'Sophie can't stop laughing when she looks at him.'

You damned dog, you're lying! You've got a wicked tongue! As if I didn't know you're jealous! And who's responsible for this? Why, the head of the department! That man has vowed undying hatred for me and does me harm whenever he has the chance. Let's see though: there's one more letter. Perhaps the explanation's there:

'*Ma chère* Fidèle, please forgive me for being so long writing to you. I have been in raptures. The author who said love is a second life was absolutely right. Great changes have been taking place in our house. The gentleman of the court comes every day now. Sophie is madly in love with him. Papa is in very high spirits. I even heard from Grigory (one of our servants who sweeps the floor and seems to be talking to himself all the time) that the wedding's going to be very soon. Papa is set on marrying off Sophie either to a general, or a court chamberlain, or a colonel ...'

Damnation! I can't read any more ... It's always noblemen or generals. All the good things in this world go to gentlemen of the court or generals. People like me scrape up a few crumbs of happiness and just as you're about to reach out to grasp them, along comes a nobleman or a general to snatch them away. Hell! I'd like to be a general, not just to win her, and all the rest of it, but to see them crawling around after me, with all their puns and high and mighty jokes from the court. Then I could tell them all to go to hell. Damn it! It's enough to make you weep. I tore that stupid little dog's letter into little bits.

December 3rd

It's impossible! What twaddle! There just *can't* be a wedding. And what if he *is* a gentleman of the court? It's only a kind of distinction conferred on you, not something that you can see, or touch with your hands. A court chamberlain doesn't have a third eye in the middle of his forehead, and his nose isn't made of gold either. It's just like mine or anyone else's: he uses it to sniff or sneeze with, but not for coughing. Several times I've tried to discover the reason for these differences. Why am I just a titular councillor?* Perhaps I'm really a count or a general and am merely imagining I'm a titular councillor? Perhaps I don't really know who I am at all? History has lots of examples of that sort of thing: there was some fairly ordinary man, not what you'd call a nobleman, but simply a tradesman or even a serf, and suddenly he discovered he was a great lord or a baron. So if a peasant can turn into someone like that, what would a nobleman become? Say, for example, I suddenly appeared in a general's uniform, with an epaulette on my left shoulder and a blue sash across my chest – what then? What tune would my beautiful young lady sing then? And Papa, our Director? Oh, he's so ambitious! He must be a mason,◊ no doubt about that, although he pretends to be this, that and the other; he only puts out two fingers to shake hands with. But surely, can't I be promoted to Governor General or Commissary or something or other this very minute? And I should like to know why I'm a titular councillor? Why precisely a *titular* councillor?

December 5th

I spent the whole morning reading the papers. Strange things are happening in Spain. I read that the throne has been left vacant and that the nobility are having a great deal of trouble choosing an heir, with the result that there's a lot of civil commotion.◊ This strikes me as very strange. They're saying some 'donna'◊ must succeed to the throne. But she can't succeed to the throne: that's impossible. A king must inherit the throne. And they say there's no king anyway. But there *must* be a king. There can't be a government without one. There's a king all right, but he's hiding in some obscure place. He must be somewhere, but is forced to stay in hiding for family reasons, or perhaps because he's in danger from some foreign country, such as France. Or there may be another explanation.

December 8th

I was about to go to the office but various reasons and considerations held me back. I couldn't get that Spanish business out of my head. How could a woman inherit the throne? They wouldn't allow it. Firstly, England wouldn't stand for it. And what's more, it would affect the whole of European policy: the Austrian Emperor, our Tsar, ... I must confess, these events shook me up so much I couldn't put my mind to anything all day. Mavra pointed out that I was very absent-minded during supper. And, in fact, in a fit of distraction I threw two plates on to the floor, and they broke immediately. After dinner I walked along a street that led downhill. Discovered nothing very edifying. Afterwards I lay on my bed for a long time and pondered the Spanish question.

April 43rd, 2000

Today is a day of great triumph. There *is* a king of Spain. He has been found at last. That king is *me*. I only discovered this today. Frankly, it all came to me in a flash. I cannot understand how I could even think or imagine for one moment I was only a titular councillor. I can't explain how such a ridiculous idea ever entered my head. Anyway, I'm rather pleased no one's thought of having me put away yet. The path ahead is clear: everything is as bright as daylight.

I don't really understand why, but before this revelation everything was enveloped in a kind of mist. And the whole reason for this, as I see it, is that people are under the misapprehension that the human brain is situated in the head: nothing could be further from the truth. It is carried by the wind from the Caspian Sea.

The first thing I did was to tell Mavra who I was. When she heard that the King of Spain was standing before her, she wrung her hands and nearly died of fright. The stupid woman had obviously *never* set eyes on the King of Spain before. However, I managed to calm her and with a few kind words tried to convince her that the new sovereign was well-disposed towards her and that I wasn't at all annoyed because she sometimes made a mess of my shoes.

But what can you expect from the common herd? You just can't converse with them about the higher things in life. Mavra was frightened because she was sure all kings of Spain looked like Philip II. But I explained that there was no resemblance between me and Philip and that I didn't have a single Capuchin friar° under my sway ... Didn't go to the office today. To hell with them! No, my friends, you won't tempt me now. I've had enough of copying out your filthy documents!

86th Martober, between day and night
One of the administrative clerks called today, saying it was time I went to the office and that I hadn't been for three weeks. So I went – just for a joke. The head clerk thought I would bow to him and start apologizing, but I gave him a cool look, not too hostile, but not too friendly either. I sat down at my desk as though no one else existed. As I looked at all that clerical scum I thought: 'If only you knew who's sitting in the same office with you ... God, what a fuss you'd make! Even the head clerk himself would start bowing and scraping, just as he does when the Director's there.' They put some papers in front of me, from which I was supposed to make an abstract. But I didn't so much as lift a finger. A few minutes later everyone was rushing round like mad. They said the Director was coming. Many of the clerks jostled each other as they tried to be first to bow to him as he came in. But I didn't budge. Everyone buttoned up his jacket as the Director walked across the office, but I didn't make a move. So he's a departmental director, what of it? He's really a *cork*, not a director. And an ordinary cork at that – a common or garden cork, and nothing else, the kind used for stopping bottles. What tickled me more than anything else was when they shoved a paper in front of me to sign. Of course, they were thinking I would sign myself as: Clerk No. So-and-so, right at the very bottom of the page. Well, let them think again! In the most important place, just where the Director puts his signature, I wrote 'Ferdinand VIII'.

The awed silence that descended on everyone was amazing; but I merely waved my hand and said: 'There's really no need for this show of loyalty,' and I walked out.

I went straight to the Director's flat. He wasn't at home. The footman wouldn't let me in at first, but what I said to him made his arms drop limply to his side. I made my way straight to *her* boudoir. She was sitting in front of the mirror and she jumped up and stepped backwards. I didn't tell her, however, that I was the King of Spain. All I said was that happiness such as she had never imagined awaited her, and that we would be together, in spite of hostile plots against us. Then I thought I'd said enough and left. But how crafty women can be! Only then did it dawn on me what they are really like. So far, no one has ever discovered whom women are in love with. I was the first to solve this mystery: they are in love with the Devil. And I'm not joking. While physicians write a lot of nonsense, saying they are this and that, the truth is, women are in love with the Devil, and no one else. Can you see that woman raising her lorgnette° in the first tier of a theatre box? Do you think she's looking at that fat man with a medal? On the contrary, she's looking at the Devil standing behind his back. Now he's hiding in the medal and is beckoning her with his finger! She'll marry him, that's for certain. And all those clerks who curry favour everywhere they go, insisting they are patriots, when all they want is money from rents! They'd sell their own mother, or father, or God for money, the crawlers, the Judases!° And all this ambition is caused by a little bubble under the tongue which contains a tiny worm about the size of a pinhead, and it's all the work of some barber living in Gorokhovaya Street. I can't remember his name for the moment but one thing I'm sure of is that with the help of an old midwife he wants to spread Mahommedanism° throughout the world. And I've already heard tell that most of the people in France are now practising the faith.

No date. The day didn't have one

I walked incognito down Nevsky Avenue. His Imperial Majesty drove past. Every single person doffed his hat, and I followed suit. However, I didn't let out that I was the King of Spain. I considered it improper to reveal my true identity right there in the middle of the crowd, because, according to etiquette, I ought first to be presented at court. So far, the only thing that had stopped me was not having any royal clothes. If only I could get hold of a cloak. I would have gone to a tailor, but they're such asses. What's more they tend to neglect their work, preferring to take part in shady transactions, and most of them end up mending the roads. I decided to have a mantle made out of my new uniform, which I'd worn only twice. I decided to make it myself, so that those crooks shouldn't ruin it, and shut myself in my room so that nobody would see. I had to cut it all up with a pair of scissors, because the style's completely different.

I don't remember the date. There wasn't any month either.
Damned if I know what it was.

The cloak is ready now. Mavra screamed when I put it on. But I still can't make up my mind whether to present myself at court. So far no deputation's arrived from Spain and it would be contrary to etiquette to go on my own. It would detract from my dignity. Anyway I'm expecting them any minute now.

The first

I'm really astonished the deputation's so slow in coming. Whatever can have held them up? Could it be France? Yes, she's extremely hostile at the moment. I went to the post office to see if there was any news about the Spanish deputation. But the postmaster was extremely stupid and knew nothing about it. 'No,' he said, 'no Spanish deputation has arrived but if you care to send a letter, it will be dispatched in the normal manner.'

To hell with it! Letters are trash. Only chemists write letters.◇

Madrid, 30th Februarius

So I'm in Spain now, and it was all so quick I hardly knew what was happening. This morning the Spanish deputation arrived and I got into a carriage with them. We drove very fast, and this struck me as most peculiar. In fact we went at such a cracking pace we were at the Spanish frontier within half an hour. But then, there are railways all over Europe now, and ships can move extremely fast. A strange country, Spain: in the first room I entered there were a lot of people with shaven heads. However, I guessed that these must either be grandees◇ or soldiers, as they're in the habit of shaving their heads over there. But the way one of the government chancellors treated me was strange in the extreme. He took me by the arm and pushed me into a small room, saying: 'Sit there, and if you call yourself King Ferdinand once more, I'll thrash that nonsense out of you.' But as I knew that this was just some sort of test I refused, for which the chancellor struck me twice on the back, so painfully that I nearly cried out. But I controlled myself, as I knew that this was the normal procedure with Spanish knights before initiating someone into a very high rank and that even now the code of chivalry is still maintained over there. Left on my own I decided to get down to government business. I have discovered that China and Spain are really one and the same country, and it's only ignorance that leads people to think that they're two different nations. If you don't believe me, then try and write 'Spain' and you'll end up writing 'China'. Apart from all this, I'm very annoyed by an event that's due to take place at 7 o'clock tomorrow. A strange phenomenon: the earth is going to land on the moon. An account of this has been written by the celebrated English chemist Wellington.

I confess I felt deeply troubled when I considered how unusually delicate and insubstantial the moon is. The moon, as everyone knows, is usually made in Hamburg, and they make a complete hash of it. I'm surprised that the English don't do something about it. The moon is manufactured by a lame cooper,* and it's obvious the idiot has no idea what it should be made of. The materials he uses are tarred rope and linseed oil. That's why there's such a terrible stink all over the earth, which makes us stop our noses up. And it also explains why the moon is such a delicate sphere, and why people can't live there – only noses. For this reason we can't see our own noses any more, as they're all on the moon. When I reflected how heavy the earth is and that our noses might be ground into the surface when it landed, I was so worried I put my socks and shoes on and hurried into the state council room to instruct the police not to let the earth land on the moon. The grandees with their shaven heads – the council chamber was chock-full of them – were a very clever lot, and as soon as I told them: 'Gentlemen, let us save the moon because the earth intends landing there,' everyone fell over himself to carry out my royal wish. Many of them went wild to reach the moon. But just at this moment in came the mighty chancellor. Everyone fled when they saw him. Being the king, I stayed where I was. But to my astonishment the chancellor hit me with his stick and drove me back into my room. That shows you how strong tradition is in Spain!

January in the same year falling after February
Up to this time Spain had been somewhat of a mystery to me. Their native customs and court etiquette are really most peculiar. I don't understand, I really do *not* understand them. Today they shaved my head even though I shrieked as loud as I could that I didn't want to be a monk. And I have only a faint memory of what happened when they poured cold water over my head. Never before had I gone through such hell. I was in such a frenzy they had difficulty in holding me down. What these strange customs mean is beyond me. So foolish, idiotic! And the utter stupidity of their kings who have still not

abolished this tradition really defeats me. After everything that's happened to me, I think I'm safe in hazarding a guess that I've fallen into the hands of the Inquisition, and the person I thought was a minister of state was really the Grand Inquisitor° himself. But I still don't understand how *kings* can be subjected to the Inquisition. It could of course be France that's putting them up to it, and I mean Polignac° in particular. What a swine he is! He's sworn to have me done away with. The whole time he's persecuting me; but I know very well, my friend, that you're led by the English. The English are acute politicians and worm their way into everything. The whole world knows that when England takes snuff, France sneezes.

The 25th

Today the Grand Inquisitor came into the room, but as soon as I heard his footsteps I hid under the table. When he saw I wasn't there, he started calling out. First he shouted: 'Poprishchin!' – I didn't say a word. Then: 'Axenty Ivanov! Titular Councillor! Nobleman!' – still I didn't reply. 'Ferdinand the Eighth, King of Spain!' I was in half a mind to stick my head out, but thought better of it. 'No, my friend, you can't fool me! I know only too well you're going to pour cold water over my head.' He spotted me all the same and drove me out from under the table with his stick. The damned thing is terribly painful. But my next discovery that every cock has its Spain, tucked away under its feathers, made up for all these torments. The Grand Inquisitor left in a very bad mood however and threatened me with some sort of punishment. But I didn't care a rap about his helpless rage, as I knew full well he was functioning like a machine, a mere tool of the English.

Da 34 te Mth eary ᴚɐqɯɐʌ 349

No, I haven't the strength to endure it any longer! Good God, what are they doing to me? They're pouring cold water over my head! They won't listen to me or come and see me. What have I done to them? Why do they torture me so? What can they want from a miserable wretch like me? What can I offer them when I've nothing of my own? I can't stand this torture any more. My head is burning and everything is spinning round and round. Save me! Take me away! Give me a troika* with horses swift as the whirlwind! Climb up, driver, and let the bells ring! Soar away, horses, and carry me from this world! Further, further, where nothing can be seen, nothing at all! Over there the sky whirls round. A little star shines in the distance; the forest rushes past with its dark trees and the moon shines above. A deep blue haze is spreading like a carpet; a guitar string twangs in the mist. On one side is the sea, on the other is Italy. And over there I can see Russian peasant huts. Is that my house looking dimly blue in the distance? And is that my mother sitting at the window? Mother, save your poor son! Shed a tear on his aching head! See how they're torturing him! Press a wretched orphan to your breast! There's no place for him in this world! They're persecuting him! Mother, have pity on your poor little child ...

And did you know that the Dhey of Algiers* has a wart right under his nose?

The Yellow Wallpaper

Charlotte Perkins Gilman

It is very seldom that mere ordinary people like John and myself secure ancestral halls for the summer.

A colonial mansion, a hereditary estate, I would say a haunted house and reach the height of romantic felicity° – but that would be asking too much of fate!

Still I will proudly declare that there is something queer about it.

Else, why should it be let so cheaply? And why have stood so long untenanted?

John laughs at me, of course, but one expects that.

John is practical in the extreme. He has no patience with faith, an intense horror of superstition, and he scoffs openly at any talk of things not to be felt and seen and put down in figures.

John is a physician, and *perhaps* – (I would not say it to a living soul, of course, but this is dead paper and a great relief to my mind) – *perhaps* that is one reason I do not get well faster.

You see, he does not believe I am sick! And what can one do?

If a physician of high standing, and one's own husband, assures friends and relatives that there is really nothing the matter with one but temporary nervous depression – a slight hysterical tendency – what is one to do?

My brother is also a physician, and also of high standing, and he says the same thing.

So I take phosphates or phosphites – whichever it is – and tonics, and air and exercise, and journeys, and am absolutely forbidden to 'work' until I am well again.

Personally, I disagree with their ideas.

Personally, I believe that congenial work, with excitement and change, would do me good.

But what is one to do?

I did write for a while in spite of them; but it *does* exhaust me a good deal – having to be so sly about it, or else meet with heavy opposition.

I sometimes fancy that in my condition, if I had less opposition and more society and stimulus – but John says the very worst thing I can do is to think about my condition, and I confess it always makes me feel bad.

So I will let it alone and talk about the house.

The most beautiful place! It is quite alone, standing well back from the road, quite three miles from the village. It makes me think of English places that you read about, for there are hedges and walls and gates that lock, and lots of separate little houses for the gardeners and people.

There is a *delicious* garden! I never saw such a garden – large and shady, full of box-bordered* paths, and lined with long grape-covered arbors with seats under them.

There were greenhouses, but they are all broken now.

There was some legal trouble, I believe, something about the heirs and co-heirs; anyhow, the place has been empty for years.

That spoils my ghostliness, I am afraid, but I don't care – there is something strange about the house – I can feel it.

I even said so to John one moonlight evening, but he said what I felt was a draught, and shut the window.

I get unreasonably angry with John sometimes. I'm sure I never used to be so sensitive. I think it is due to this nervous condition.

But John says if I feel so I shall neglect proper self-control; so I take pains to control myself – before him, at least, and that makes me very tired.

I don't like our room a bit. I wanted one downstairs that opened onto the piazza and had roses all over the window, and such pretty old-fashioned chintz hangings! But John would not hear of it.

He said there was only one window and not room for two beds, and no near room for him if he took another.

He is very careful and loving, and hardly lets me stir without special direction.

I have a schedule prescription for each hour in the day; he takes all care from me, and so I feel basely ungrateful not to value it more.

He said he came here solely on my account, that I was to have perfect rest and all the air I could get. 'Your exercise depends on your strength, my dear,' said he, 'and your food somewhat on your appetite; but air you can absorb all the time.' So we took the nursery at the top of the house.

It is a big, airy room, the whole floor nearly, with windows that look all ways, and air and sunshine galore. It was nursery first, and then playroom and gymnasium, I should judge, for the windows are barred for little children, and there are rings and things in the walls.

The paint and paper look as if a boys' school had used it. It is stripped off – the paper – in great patches all around the head of my bed, about as far as I can reach, and in a great place on the other side of the room low down. I never saw a worse paper in my life. One of those sprawling, flamboyant patterns committing every artistic sin.

It is dull enough to confuse the eye in following, pronounced enough constantly to irritate and provoke study, and when you follow the lame uncertain curves for a little distance they suddenly commit suicide – plunge off at outrageous angles, destroy themselves in unheard-of contradictions.

The color is repellent, almost revolting: a smouldering unclean yellow, strangely faded by the slow-turning sunlight. It is a dull yet lurid orange in some places, a sickly sulphur tint in others.

No wonder the children hated it! I should hate it myself if I had to live in this room long.

There comes John, and I must put this away – he hates to have me write a word.

We have been here two weeks, and I haven't felt like writing before, since that first day.

I am sitting by the window now, up in this atrocious nursery, and there is nothing to hinder my writing as much as I please, save lack of strength.

John is away all day, and even some nights when his cases are serious.

I am glad my case is not serious!

But these nervous troubles are dreadfully depressing.

John does not know how much I really suffer. He knows there is no reason to suffer, and that satisfies him.

Of course it is only nervousness. It does weigh on me so not to do my duty in any way!

I meant to be such a help to John, such a real rest and comfort, and here I am a comparative burden already!

Nobody would believe what an effort it is to do what little I am able – to dress and entertain, and order things.

It is fortunate Mary is so good with the baby. Such a dear baby!

And yet I *cannot* be with him, it makes me so nervous.

I suppose John never was nervous in his life. He laughs at me so about this wallpaper!

At first he meant to repaper the room, but afterward he said that I was letting it get the better of me, and that nothing was worse for a nervous patient than to give way to such fancies.

He said that after the wallpaper was changed it would be the heavy bedstead, and then the barred windows, and then that gate at the head of the stairs, and so on.

'You know the place is doing you good,' he said, 'and really, dear, I don't care to renovate the house just for a three months' rental.'

'Then do let us go downstairs,' I said. 'There are such pretty rooms there.'

Then he took me in his arms and called me a blessed little goose, and said he would go down the cellar, if I wished, and have it whitewashed into the bargain.

But he is right enough about the beds and windows and things.

It is as airy and comfortable a room as anyone need wish, and, of course, I would not be so silly as to make him uncomfortable just for a whim.

I'm really getting quite fond of the big room, all but that horrid paper.

Out of one window I can see the garden – those mysterious deep-shaded arbors, the riotous old-fashioned flowers, and bushes and gnarly trees.

Out of another I get a lovely view of the bay and a little private wharf° belonging to the estate. There is a beautiful shaded lane that runs down there from the house. I always fancy I see people walking in these numerous paths and arbors, but John has cautioned me not to give way to fancy in the least. He says that with my imaginative power and habit of story-making, a nervous weakness like mine is sure to lead to all manner of excited fancies, and that I ought to use my will and good sense to check the tendency. So I try.

I think sometimes that if I were only well enough to write a little it would relieve the press of ideas and rest me.

But I find I get pretty tired when I try.

It is so discouraging not to have any advice and companion-ship about my work. When I get really well, John says we will ask Cousin Henry and Julia down for a long visit; but he says he would as soon put fireworks in my pillow-case as to let me have those stimulating people about now.

I wish I could get well faster.

But I must not think about that. This paper looks to me as if it *knew* what a vicious influence it had!

There is a recurrent spot where the pattern lolls like a broken neck and two bulbous eyes stare at you upside down.

I get positively angry with the impertinence of it and the everlastingness. Up and down and sideways they crawl, and those absurd unblinking eyes are everywhere. There is one place where two breadths didn't match, and the eyes go all up and down the line, one a little higher than the other.

I never saw so much expression in an inanimate thing before, and we all know how much expression they have! I used to lie awake as a child and get more entertainment and terror out of blank walls and plain furniture than most children could find in a toy-store.

I remember what a kindly wink the knobs of our big old bureau used to have, and there was one chair that always seemed like a strong friend.

I used to feel that if any of the other things looked too fierce I could always hop into that chair and be safe.

The furniture in this room is no worse than inharmonious, however, for we had to bring it all from downstairs. I suppose when this was used as a playroom they had to take the nursery things out, and no wonder! I never saw such ravages as the children have made here.

The wallpaper, as I said before, is torn off in spots, and it sticketh closer than a brother – they must have had perseverance as well as hatred.

Then the floor is scratched and gouged and splintered, the plaster itself is dug out here and there, and this great heavy bed, which is all we found in the room, looks as if it had been through the wars.

But I don't mind it a bit – only the paper.

There comes John's sister. Such a dear girl as she is, and so careful of me! I must not let her find me writing.

She is a perfect and enthusiastic housekeeper, and hopes for no better profession. I verily believe she thinks it is the writing which made me sick!

But I can write when she is out, and see her a long way off from these windows.

There is one that commands the road, a lovely shaded winding road, and one that just looks off over the country. A lovely country, too, full of great elms and velvet meadows.

This wallpaper has a kind of sub-pattern in a different shade, a particularly irritating one, for you can only see it in certain lights, and not clearly then.

But in the places where it isn't faded and where the sun is just so – I can see a strange, provoking, formless sort of figure that seems to skulk about behind that silly and conspicuous front design.

There's sister on the stairs!

Well, the Fourth of July° is over! The people are all gone, and I am tired out. John thought it might do me good to see a little company, so we just had Mother and Nellie and the children down for a week.

Of course I didn't do a thing. Jennie sees to everything now.

But it tired me all the same.

John says if I don't pick up faster he shall send me to Weir Mitchell° in the fall.

But I don't want to go there at all. I had a friend who was in his hands once, and she says he is just like John and my brother, only more so!

Besides, it is such an undertaking to go so far.

I don't feel as if it was worthwhile to turn my hand over for anything, and I'm getting dreadfully fretful and querulous.

I cry at nothing, and cry most of the time.

Of course I don't when John is here, or anybody else, but when I am alone.

And I am alone a good deal just now. John is kept in town very often by serious cases, and Jennie is good and lets me alone when I want her to.

So I walk a little in the garden or down that lovely lane, sit on the porch under the roses, and lie down up here a good deal.

I'm getting really fond of the room in spite of the wallpaper. Perhaps *because* of the wallpaper.

It dwells in my mind so!

I lie here on this great immovable bed – it is nailed down, I believe – and follow that pattern about by the hour. It is as good as gymnastics, I assure you. I start, we'll say, at the bottom, down in the corner over there where it has not been touched, and I determine for the thousandth time that I *will* follow that pointless pattern to some sort of a conclusion.

I know a little of the principle of design, and I know this thing was not arranged on any laws of radiation, or alternation; or repetition, or symmetry, or anything else that I ever heard of.

It is repeated, of course, by the breadths, but not otherwise.

Looked at in one way, each breadth stands alone; the bloated curves and flourishes – a kind of 'debased Romanesque'◊ with delirium tremens◊ – go waddling up and down in isolated columns of fatuity.◊

But, on the other hand, they connect diagonally, and the sprawling outlines run off in great slanting waves of optic horror, like a lot of wallowing sea-weeds in full chase.

The whole thing goes horizontally, too, at least it seems so, and I exhaust myself trying to distinguish the order of its going in that direction.

They have used a horizontal breadth for a frieze,◊ and that adds wonderfully to the confusion.

There is one end of the room where it is almost intact, and there, when the crosslights fade and the low sun shines directly upon it, I can almost fancy radiation after all – the interminable grotesque seems to form around a common center and rush off in headlong plunges of equal distraction.

It makes me tired to follow it. I will take a nap, I guess.

I don't know why I should write this.

I don't want to.

I don't feel able.

And I know John would think it absurd. But I *must* say what I feel and think in some way – it is such a relief!

But the effort is getting to be greater than the relief.

Half the time now I am awfully lazy, and lie down ever so much. John says I mustn't lose my strength, and has me take cod liver oil and lots of tonics and things, to say nothing of ale and wine and rare meat.

Dear John! He loves me very dearly, and hates to have me sick. I tried to have a real earnest reasonable talk with him the other day, and tell him how I wish he would let me go and make a visit to Cousin Henry and Julia.

But he said I wasn't able to go, nor able to stand it after I got there; and I did not make out a very good case for myself, for I was crying before I had finished.

It is getting to be a great effort for me to think straight. Just this nervous weakness, I suppose.

And dear John gathered me up in his arms, and just carried me upstairs and laid me on the bed, and sat by me and read to me till it tired my head.

He said I was his darling and his comfort and all he had, and that I must take care of myself for his sake, and keep well.

He says no one but myself can help me out of it, that I must use my will and self-control and not let any silly fancies run away with me.

There's one comfort – the baby is well and happy, and does not have to occupy this nursery with the horrid wallpaper.

If we had not used it, that blessed child would have! What a fortunate escape! Why, I wouldn't have a child of mine, an impressionable little thing, live in such a room for worlds.

I never thought of it before, but it is lucky that John kept me here after all; I can stand it so much easier than a baby, you see.

Of course I never mention it to them any more – I am too wise – but I keep watch for it all the same.

There are things in that wallpaper that nobody knows about but me, or ever will.

Behind that outside pattern the dim shapes get clearer every day.

It is always the same shape, only very numerous.

And it is like a woman stooping down and creeping about behind that pattern. I don't like it a bit. I wonder – I begin to think – I wish John would take me away from here!

It is so hard to talk with John about my case, because he is so wise, and because he loves me so.

But I tried it last night.

It was moonlight. The moon shines in all around just as the sun does.

I hate to see it sometimes, it creeps so slowly, and always comes in by one window or another.

John was asleep and I hated to waken him, so I kept still and watched the moonlight on that undulating wallpaper till I felt creepy.

The faint figure behind seemed to shake the pattern, just as if she wanted to get out.

I got up softly and went to feel and see if the paper *did* move, and when I came back John was awake.

'What is it, little girl?' he said. 'Don't go walking about like that – you'll get cold.'

I thought it was a good time to talk, so I told him that I really was not gaining here, and that I wished he would take me away.

'Why, darling!' said he. 'Our lease will be up in three weeks, and I can't see how to leave before.

'The repairs are not done at home, and I cannot possibly leave town just now. Of course, if you were in any danger, I could and would, but you really are better, dear, whether you can see it or not. I am a doctor, dear, and I know. You are gaining flesh and color, your appetite is better, I feel really much easier about you.'

'I don't weigh a bit more,' said I, 'nor as much; and my appetite may be better in the evening when you are here but it is worse in the morning when you are away!'

'Bless her little heart!' said he with a big hug. 'She shall be as sick as she pleases! But now let's improve the shining hours by going to sleep, and talk about it in the morning!'

'And you won't go away?' I asked gloomily.

'Why, how can I, dear? It is only three weeks more and then we will take a nice little trip of a few days while Jennie is getting the house ready. Really, dear, you are better!'

'Better in body perhaps – ' I began, and stopped short, for he sat up straight and looked at me with such a stern, reproachful look that I could not say another word.

'My darling,' said he, 'I beg of you, for my sake and for our child's sake, as well as for your own, that you will never for one instant let that idea enter your mind! There is nothing so dangerous, so fascinating, to a temperament like yours. It is a false and foolish fancy. Can you not trust me as a physician when I tell you so?'

So of course I said no more on that score, and we went to sleep before long. He thought I was asleep first, but I wasn't, and lay there for hours trying to decide whether that front pattern and the back pattern really did move together or separately.

On a pattern like this, by daylight, there is a lack of sequence, a defiance of law, that is a constant irritant to a normal mind.

The color is hideous enough, and unreliable enough, and infuriating enough, but the pattern is torturing.

You think you have mastered it, but just as you get well under way in following, it turns a back-somersault and there you are. It slaps you in the face, knocks you down, and tramples upon you. It is like a bad dream.

The outside pattern is a florid arabesque,° reminding one of a fungus. If you can imagine a toadstool in joints, an interminable string of toadstools, budding and sprouting in endless convolutions – why, that is something like it.

That is, sometimes!

There is one marked peculiarity about this paper, a thing nobody seems to notice but myself, and that is that it changes as the light changes.

When the sun shoots in through the east window – I always watch for that first long, straight ray – it changes so quickly that I never can quite believe it.

That is why I watch it always.

By moonlight – the moon shines in all night when there is a moon – I wouldn't know it was the same paper.

At night in any kind of light, in twilight, candlelight, lamplight, and worst of all by moonlight, it becomes bars! The outside pattern, I mean, and the woman behind it is as plain as can be.

I didn't realize for a long time what the thing was that showed behind, that dim sub-pattern, but now I am quite sure it is a woman.

By daylight she is subdued, quiet. I fancy it is the pattern that keeps her so still. It is so puzzling. It keeps me quiet by the hour.

I lie down ever so much now. John says it is good for me, and to sleep all I can.

Indeed he started the habit by making me lie down for an hour after each meal.

It is a very bad habit, I am convinced, for you see, I don't sleep.

And that cultivates deceit, for I don't tell them I'm awake – oh, no!

The fact is I am getting a little afraid of John.

He seems very queer sometimes, and even Jennie has an inexplicable look.

It strikes me occasionally, just as a scientific hypothesis, that perhaps it is the paper!

I have watched John when he did not know I was looking, and come into the room suddenly on the most innocent excuses, and I've caught him several times *looking at the paper!* And Jennie too. I caught Jennie with her hand on it once.

She didn't know I was in the room, and when I asked her in a quiet, a very quiet voice, with the most restrained manner possible, what she was doing with the paper, she turned around as if she had been caught stealing, and looked quite angry – asked me why I should frighten her so!

Then she said that the paper stained everything it touched, that she had found yellow smooches on all my clothes and John's and she wished we would be more careful!

Did not that sound innocent? But I know she was studying that pattern, and I am determined that nobody shall find it out but myself!

Life is very much more exciting now than it used to be. You see, I have something more to expect, to look forward to, to watch. I really do eat better, and am more quiet than I was.

John is so pleased to see me improve! He laughed a little the other day, and said I seemed to be flourishing in spite of my wallpaper.

I turned it off with a laugh. I had no intention of telling him it was *because* of the wallpaper – he would make fun of me. He might even want to take me away.

I don't want to leave now until I have found it out. There is a week more, and I think that will be enough.

I'm feeling so much better!

I don't sleep much at night, for it is so interesting to watch developments; but I sleep a good deal during the daytime.

In the daytime it is tiresome and perplexing.

There are always new shoots on the fungus, and new shades of yellow all over it. I cannot keep count of them, though I have tried conscientiously.

It is the strangest yellow, that wallpaper! It makes me think of all the yellow things I ever saw – not beautiful ones like buttercups, but old, foul, bad yellow things.

But there is something else about that paper – the smell! I noticed it the moment we came into the room, but with so much air and sun it was not bad. Now we have had a week of fog and rain, and whether the windows are open or not, the smell is here.

It creeps all over the house.

I find it hovering in the dining-room, skulking in the parlor, hiding in the hall, lying in wait for me on the stairs.

It gets into my hair.

Even when I go to ride, if I turn my head suddenly and surprise it – there is that smell!

Such a peculiar odor, too! I have spent hours in trying to analyze it, to find what it smelled like.

It is not bad – at first – and very gentle, but quite the subtlest, most enduring odor I ever met.

In this damp weather it is awful. I wake up in the night and find it hanging over me.

It used to disturb me at first. I thought seriously of burning the house – to reach the smell.

But now I am used to it. The only thing I can think of that it is like is the *color* of the paper! A yellow smell.

There is a very funny mark on this wall, low down, near the mopboard.° A streak that runs round the room. It goes behind every piece of furniture, except the bed, a long, straight, even *smooch*, as if it had been rubbed over and over.

I wonder how it was done and who did it, and what they did it for. Round and round and round – round and round and round – it makes me dizzy!

I really have discovered something at last.

Through watching so much at night, when it changes so, I have finally found out.

The front pattern *does* move – and no wonder! The woman behind shakes it!

Sometimes I think there are a great many women behind, and sometimes only one, and she crawls around fast, and her crawling shakes it all over.

Then in the very bright spots she keeps still, and in the very shady spots she just takes hold of the bars and shakes them hard.

And she is all the time trying to climb through. But nobody could climb through that pattern – it strangles so; I think that is why it has so many heads.

They get through, and then the pattern strangles them off and turns them upside down, and makes their eyes white!

If those heads were covered or taken off it would not be half so bad.

I think that woman gets out in the daytime!

And I'll tell you why – privately – I've seen her!

I can see her out of every one of my windows!

It is the same woman, I know, for she is always creeping, and most women do not creep by daylight.

I see her in that long shaded lane, creeping up and down. I see her in those dark grape arbors, creeping all around the garden.

I see her on that long road under the trees, creeping along, and when a carriage comes she hides under the blackberry vines.

I don't blame her a bit. It must be very humiliating to be caught creeping by daylight!

I always lock the door when I creep by daylight. I can't do it at night, for I know John would suspect something at once.

And John is so queer now that I don't want to irritate him. I wish he would take another room! Besides, I don't want anybody to get that woman out at night but myself.

I often wonder if I could see her out of all the windows at once.

But, turn as fast as I can, I can only see out of one at one time.

And though I always see her, she *may* be able to creep faster than I can turn! I have watched her sometimes away off in the open country, creeping as fast as a cloud shadow in a wind.

If only that top pattern could be gotten off from the under one! I mean to try it, little by little.

I have found out another funny thing, but I shan't tell it this time! It does not do to trust people too much.

There are only two more days to get this paper off, and I believe John is beginning to notice. I don't like the look in his eyes.

And I heard him ask Jennie a lot of professional questions about me. She had a very good report to give.

She said I slept a good deal in the daytime.

John knows I don't sleep very well at night, for all I'm so quiet!

He asked me all sorts of questions, too, and pretended to be very loving and kind.

As if I couldn't see through him!

Still, I don't wonder he acts so, sleeping under this paper for three months.

It only interests me, but I feel sure John and Jennie are affected by it.

Hurrah! This is the last day, but it is enough. John is to stay in town over night, and won't be out until this evening.

Jennie wanted to sleep with me – the sly thing; but I told her I should undoubtedly rest better for a night all alone.

That was clever, for really I wasn't alone a bit! As soon as it was moonlight and that poor thing began to crawl and shake the pattern, I got up and ran to help her.

I pulled and she shook. I shook and she pulled, and before morning we had peeled off yards of that paper.

A strip about as high as my head and half around the room.

And then when the sun came and that awful pattern began to laugh at me, I declared I would finish it today!

We go away tomorrow, and they are moving all my furniture down again to leave things as they were before.

Jennie looked at the wall in amazement, but I told her merrily that I did it out of pure spite at the vicious thing.

She laughed and said she wouldn't mind doing it herself, but I must not get tired.

How she betrayed herself that time!

But I am here, and no person touches this paper but Me – not *alive*!

She tried to get me out of the room – it was too patent! But I said it was so quiet and empty and clean now that I believed I would lie down again and sleep all I could, and not to wake me even for dinner – I would call when I woke.

So now she is gone, and the servants are gone, and the things are gone, and there is nothing left but that great bedstead nailed down, with the canvas mattress we found on it.

We shall sleep downstairs tonight, and take the boat home tomorrow.

I quite enjoy the room, now it is bare again.

How those children did tear about here!

This bedstead is fairly gnawed!

But I must get to work.

I have locked the door and thrown the key down into the front path.

I don't want to go out, and I don't want to have anybody come in, till John comes.

I want to astonish him.

I've got a rope up here that even Jennie did not find. If that woman does get out, and tries to get away, I can tie her!

But I forgot I could not reach far without anything to stand on!

This bed will *not* move!

I tried to lift and push it until I was lame, and then I got so angry I bit off a little piece at one corner – but it hurt my teeth.

Then I peeled off all the paper I could reach standing on the floor. It sticks horribly and the pattern just enjoys it! All those strangled heads and bulbous eyes and waddling fungus growths just shriek with derision!

I am getting angry enough to do something desperate. To jump out of the window would be admirable exercise, but the bars are too strong even to try.

Besides I wouldn't do it. Of course not. I know well enough that a step like that is improper and might be misconstrued.

I don't like to *look* out of the windows even – there are so many of those creeping women, and they creep so fast.

I wonder if they all come out of that wallpaper as I did?

But I am securely fastened now by my well-hidden rope – you don't get *me* out in the road there!

I suppose I shall have to get back behind the pattern when it comes night, and that is hard!

It is so pleasant to be out in this great room and creep around as I please!

I don't want to go outside. I won't, even if Jennie asks me to.

For outside you have to creep on the ground, and everything is green instead of yellow.

But here I can creep smoothly on the floor, and my shoulder just fits in that long smooch around the wall, so I cannot lose my way.

Why, there's John at the door!

It is no use, young man, you can't open it!

How he does call and pound!

Now he's crying to Jennie for an axe.

It would be a shame to break down that beautiful door!

'John, dear!' said I in the gentlest voice. 'The key is down by the front steps, under a plantain° leaf!'

That silenced him for a few moments.

Then he said, very quietly indeed, 'Open the door, my darling!'

'I can't,' said I. 'The key is down by the front door under a plantain leaf!' And then I said it again, several times, very gently and slowly, and said it so often that he had to go and see, and he got it of course, and came in. He stopped short by the door.

'What is the matter?' he cried. 'For God's sake, what are you doing!'

I kept on creeping just the same, but I looked at him over my shoulder.

'I've got out at last,' said I, 'in spite of you and Jane. And I've pulled off most of the paper, so you can't put me back!'

Now why should that man have fainted? But he did, and right across my path by the wall, so that I had to creep over him every time!

Popular Mechanics

Raymond Carver

Early that day the weather turned and the snow was melting into dirty water. Streaks of it ran down from the little shoulder-high window that faced the backyard. Cars slushed by on the street outside, where it was getting dark. But it was getting dark on the inside too.

He was in the bedroom pushing clothes into a suitcase when she came to the door.

I'm glad you're leaving! I'm glad you're leaving! she said. Do you hear?

He kept on putting his things into the suitcase.

Son of a bitch! I'm so glad you're leaving! She began to cry. You can't even look me in the face, can you?

Then she noticed the baby's picture on the bed and picked it up.

He looked at her and she wiped her eyes and stared at him before turning and going back to the living room.

Bring that back, he said.

Just get your things and get out, she said.

He did not answer. He fastened the suitcase, put on his coat, looked around the bedroom before turning off the light. Then he went out to the living room.

She stood in the doorway of the little kitchen, holding the baby.

I want the baby, he said.

Are you crazy?

No, but I want the baby. I'll get someone to come by for his things.

You're not touching this baby, she said.

The baby had begun to cry and she uncovered the blanket from around his head.

Oh, oh, she said, looking at the baby.

He moved toward her.

For God's sake! she said. She took a step back into the kitchen.

I want the baby.

Get out of here!

She turned and tried to hold the baby over in a corner behind the stove.

But he came up. He reached across the stove and tightened his hands on the baby.

Let go of him, he said.

Get away, get away! she cried.

The baby was red-faced and screaming. In the scuffle they knocked down a flowerpot that hung behind the stove.

He crowded her into the wall then, trying to break her grip. He held on to the baby and pushed with all his weight.

Let go of him, he said.

Don't, she said. You're hurting the baby, she said.

I'm not hurting the baby, he said.

The kitchen window gave no light. In the near-dark he worked on her fisted fingers with one hand and with the other hand he gripped the screaming baby up under an arm near the shoulder.

She felt her fingers being forced open. She felt the baby going from her.

No! she screamed just as her hands came loose.

She would have it, this baby. She grabbed for the baby's other arm. She caught the baby around the wrist and leaned back.

But he would not let go. He felt the baby slipping out of his hands and he pulled back very hard.

In this manner, the issue was decided.

A Rose for Emily

William Faulkner

When Miss Emily Grierson died, our whole town went to her funeral: the men through a sort of respectful affection for a fallen monument, the women mostly out of curiosity to see the inside of her house, which no one save an old manservant – a combined gardener and cook – had seen in at least ten years.

It was a big, squarish frame house that had once been white, decorated with cupolas° and spires and scrolled° balconies in the heavily lightsome style of the seventies, set on what had once been our most select street. But garages and cotton gins° had encroached and obliterated even the august° names of that neighborhood; only Miss Emily's house was left, lifting its stubborn and coquettish decay above the cotton wagons and the gasoline pumps – an eyesore among eyesores. And now Miss Emily had gone to join the representatives of those august names where they lay in the cedar-bemused cemetery among the ranked and anonymous graves of Union and Confederate soldiers° who fell at the battle of Jefferson.°

Alive, Miss Emily had been a tradition, a duty, and a care; a sort of hereditary obligation upon the town, dating from that day in 1894 when Colonel Sartoris, the mayor – he who fathered the edict that no Negro woman should appear on the streets without an apron – remitted her taxes, the dispensation dating from the death of her father on into perpetuity.° Not that Miss Emily would have accepted charity. Colonel Sartoris invented an involved tale to the effect that Miss Emily's father had loaned money to the town, which the town, as a matter of business, preferred this way of repaying. Only a man of

Colonel Sartoris' generation and thought could have invented it, and only a woman could have believed it.

When the next generation, with its more modern ideas, became mayors and aldermen, this arrangement created some little dissatisfaction. On the first of the year they mailed her a tax notice. February came, and there was no reply. They wrote her a formal letter, asking her to call at the sheriff's office at her convenience. A week later the mayor wrote her himself, offering to call or to send his car for her, and received in reply a note on paper of an archaic shape, in a thin, flowing calligraphy◊ in faded ink, to the effect that she no longer went out at all. The tax notice was also enclosed, without comment.

They called a special meeting of the Board of Aldermen.◊ A deputation waited upon her, knocked at the door through which no visitor had passed since she ceased giving china-painting lessons eight or ten years earlier. They were admitted by the old Negro into a dim hall from which a stairway mounted into still more shadow. It smelled of dust and disuse – a close, dank smell. The Negro led them into the parlor. It was furnished in heavy, leather-covered furniture. When the Negro opened the blinds of one window, they could see that the leather was cracked; and when they sat down, a faint dust rose sluggishly about their thighs, spinning with slow motes in the single sunray. On a tarnished gilt easel before the fireplace stood a crayon portrait of Miss Emily's father.

They rose when she entered – a small, fat woman in black, with a thin gold chain descending to her waist and vanishing into her belt, leaning on an ebony cane with a tarnished gold head. Her skeleton was small and spare; perhaps that was why what would have been merely plumpness in another was obesity in her. She looked bloated, like a body long submerged in motionless water, and of that pallid hue. Her eyes, lost in the fatty ridges of her face, looked like two small pieces of coal pressed into a lump of dough as they moved from one face to another while the visitors stated their errand.

She did not ask them to sit. She just stood in the door and listened quietly until the spokesman came to a stumbling halt. Then they could hear the invisible watch ticking at the end of the gold chain.

Her voice was dry and cold. 'I have no taxes in Jefferson. Colonel Sartoris explained it to me. Perhaps one of you can gain access to the city records and satisfy yourselves.'

'But we have. We are the city authorities, Miss Emily. Didn't you get a notice from the sheriff, signed by him?'

'I received a paper, yes,' Miss Emily said. 'Perhaps he considers himself the sheriff. ... I have no taxes in Jefferson.'

'But there is nothing on the books to show that, you see. We must go by the – '

'See Colonel Sartoris. I have no taxes in Jefferson.'

'But, Miss Emily – '

'See Colonel Sartoris.' (Colonel Sartoris had been dead almost ten years.) 'I have no taxes in Jefferson. Tobe!' The Negro appeared. 'Show these gentlemen out.'

II

So she vanquished them, horse and foot, just as she had vanquished their fathers thirty years before about the smell. That was two years after her father's death and a short time after her sweetheart – the one we believed would marry her – had deserted her. After her father's death she went out very little; after her sweetheart went away, people hardly saw her at all. A few of the ladies had the temerity◊ to call, but were not received, and the only sign of life about the place was the Negro man – a young man then – going in and out with a market basket.

'Just as if a man – any man – could keep a kitchen properly,' the ladies said; so they were not surprised when the smell developed. It was another link between the gross, teeming world and the high and mighty Griersons.

A neighbor, a woman, complained to the mayor, Judge Stevens, eighty years old.

'But what will you have me to do about it, madam?' he said.

'Why send her word to stop it,' the woman said. 'Isn't there a law?'

'I'm sure that won't be necessary,' Judge Stevens said. 'It's probably just a snake or a rat that nigger of hers killed in the yard. I'll speak to him about it.'

The next day he received two more complaints, one from a man who came in diffident deprecation. 'We really must do something about it, Judge. I'd be the last one in the world to bother Miss Emily, but we've got to do something.' That night the Board of Aldermen met – three graybeards and one younger man, a member of the rising generation.

'It's simple enough,' he said. 'Send her word to have her place cleaned up. Give her a certain time to do it in, and if she don't … '

'Dammit, sir,' Judge Stevens said, 'will you accuse a lady to her face of smelling bad?'

So the next night, after midnight, four men crossed Miss Emily's lawn and slunk about the house like burglars, sniffing along the base of the brickwork and at the cellar openings while one of them performed a regular sowing motion with his hand out of a sack slung from his shoulder. They broke open the cellar door and sprinkled lime there, and in all the outbuildings. As they recrossed the lawn, a window that had been dark was lighted and Miss Emily sat in it, the light behind her, and her upright torso motionless as that of an idol. They crept quietly across the lawn and into the shadow of the locusts° that lined the street. After a week or two the smell went away.

That was when people had begun to feel really sorry for her. People in our town, remembering how old lady Wyatt, her great-aunt, had gone completely crazy at last, believed that the Griersons held themselves a little too high for what they really were. None of the young men were quite good enough for Miss

Emily and such. We had long thought of them as a tableau; Miss Emily a slender figure in white in the background, her father a spraddled° silhouette in the foreground, his back to her and clutching a horsewhip, the two of them framed by the back-flung front door. So when she got to be thirty and was still single, we were not pleased exactly, but vindicated; even with insanity in the family she wouldn't have turned down all of her chances if they had really materialized.

When her father died, it got about that the house was all that was left to her; and in a way, people were glad. At last they could pity Miss Emily. Being left alone, and a pauper, she had become humanized. Now she too would know the old thrill and the old despair of a penny more or less.°

The day after his death all the ladies prepared to call at the house and offer condolence and aid, as is our custom. Miss Emily met them at the door, dressed as usual and with no trace of grief on her face. She told them that her father was not dead. She did that for three days, with the ministers calling on her, and the doctors, trying to persuade her to let them dispose of the body. Just as they were about to resort to law and force, she broke down, and they buried her father quickly.

We did not say she was crazy then. We believed she had to do that. We remembered all the young men her father had driven away, and we knew that with nothing left, she would have to cling to that which had robbed her, as people will.

III

She was sick for a long time. When we saw her again, her hair was cut short, making her look like a girl, with a vague resemblance to those angels in colored church windows – sort of tragic and serene.

The town had just let the contracts for paving the sidewalks, and in the summer after her father's death they began the work. The construction company came with niggers and mules and machinery, and a foreman named Homer Barron, a Yankee$^\diamond$ – a big, dark, ready man, with a big voice and eyes lighter than his face. The little boys would follow in groups to hear him cuss the niggers, and the niggers singing in time to the rise and fall of picks. Pretty soon he knew everybody in town. Whenever you heard a lot of laughing anywhere about the square, Homer Barron would he in the center of the group. Presently we began to see him and Miss Emily on Sunday afternoons driving in the yellow-wheeled buggy and the matched team of bays from the livery stable.$^\diamond$

At first we were glad that Miss Emily would have an interest, because the ladies all said, 'Of course a Grierson would not think seriously of a Northerner, a day laborer.' But there were still others, older people, who said that even grief could not cause a real lady to forget *noblesse oblige*$^\diamond$ – without calling it *noblesse oblige*. They just said, 'Poor Emily. Her kinsfolk should come to her.' She had some kin in Alabama; but years ago her father had fallen out with them over the estate of old lady Wyatt, the crazy woman, and there was no communication between the two families. They had not even been represented at the funeral.

And as soon as the old people said, 'Poor Emily,' the whispering began. 'Do you suppose it's really so?' they said to one another. 'Of course it is. What else could … ' This behind their hands; rustling of craned$^\diamond$ silk and satin behind jalousies$^\diamond$ closed upon the sun of Sunday afternoon as the thin, swift clop-clop-clop of the matched team passed: 'Poor Emily.'

She carried her head high enough – even when we believed that she was fallen. It was as if she demanded more than ever the recognition of her dignity as the last Grierson; as if it had wanted that touch of earthiness to reaffirm her imperviousness.$^\diamond$ Like when she bought the rat poison, the arsenic. That was over a year after they had begun to say 'Poor Emily,' and while the two female cousins were visiting her.

'I want some poison,' she said to the druggist. She was over thirty then, still a slight woman, though thinner than usual, with cold, haughty black eyes in a face the flesh of which was strained across the temples and about the eye-sockets as you imagine a lighthousekeeper's face ought to look. 'I want some poison,' she said.

'Yes, Miss Emily. What kind? For rats and such? I'd recom–'

'I want the best you have. I don't care what kind.'

The druggist named several. 'They'll kill anything up to an elephant. But what you want is–'

'Arsenic,' Miss Emily said. 'Is that a good one?'

'Is … arsenic? Yes, ma'am. But what you want–'

'I want arsenic.'

The druggist looked down at her. She looked back at him, erect, her face like a strained flag. 'Why, of course,' the druggist said. 'If that's what you want. But the law requires you to tell what you are going to use it for.'

Miss Emily just stared at him her head tilted back in order to look him eye for eye, until he looked away and went and got the arsenic and wrapped it up. The Negro delivery boy brought her the package; the druggist didn't come back. When she opened the package at home there was written on the box, under the skull and bones: 'For rats.'

IV

So the next day we all said, 'She will kill herself'; and we said it would be the best thing. When she had first begun to be seen with Homer Barron, we had said, 'She will marry him.' Then we said, 'She will persuade him yet,' because Homer himself had remarked – he liked men, and it was known that he drank with younger men in the Elk's Club – that he was not a marrying man. Later we said, 'Poor Emily,' behind the jalousies as they passed on Sunday afternoon in the glittering buggy, Miss Emily with her head high and Homer Barron with his hat cocked and a cigar in his teeth, reins and whip in a yellow glove.

Then some of the ladies began to say that it was a disgrace to the town and a bad example to the young people. The men did not want to interfere, but at last the ladies forced the Baptist minister – Miss Emily's people were Episcopal* – to call upon her. He would never divulge what happened during that interview, but he refused to go back again. The next Sunday they again drove about the streets, and the following day the minister's wife wrote to Miss Emily's relations in Alabama.

So she had blood-kin under her roof again and we sat back to watch developments. At first nothing happened. Then we were sure that they were to be married. We learned that Miss Emily had been to the jeweler's and ordered a man's toilet set in silver, with the letters H.B. on each piece. Two days later we learned that she had bought a complete outfit of men's clothing, including a nightshirt, and we said, 'They are married.' We were really glad. We were glad because the two female cousins were even more Grierson than Miss Emily had ever been.

So we were not surprised when Homer Barron – the streets had been finished some time since – was gone. We were a little disappointed that there was not a public blowing-off, but we believed that he had gone on to prepare for Miss Emily's coming, or to give her a chance to get rid of the cousins. (By that time it was a cabal,* and we were all Miss Emily's allies to help circumvent the cousins.) Sure enough, after another week they departed. And, as we had expected all along, within three days Homer Barron was back in town. A neighbor saw her Negro man admit him at the kitchen door at dusk one evening.

And that was the last we saw of Homer Barron. And of Miss Emily for some time. The Negro man went in and out with the market basket, but the front door remained closed. Now and then we would see her at a window for a moment, as the men did that night when they sprinkled the lime, but for almost six months she did not appear on the streets. Then we knew that this was to be expected too; as if that quality of her father which had thwarted her woman's life so many times had been too virulent and too furious to die.

When we next saw Miss Emily, she had grown fat and her hair was turning gray. During the next few years it grew grayer and grayer until it attained an even pepper-and-salt iron-gray, when it ceased turning. Up to the day of her death at seventy-four it was still that vigorous iron-gray, like the hair of an active man.

From that time on her front door remained closed, save for a period of six or seven years, when she was about forty, during which she gave lessons in china-painting. She fitted up a studio in one of the downstairs rooms, where the daughters and granddaughters of Colonel Sartoris' contemporaries were sent to her with the same regularity and in the same spirit that they were sent on Sundays with a twenty-five cent piece for the collection plate. Meanwhile her taxes had been remitted.

Then the newer generation became the backbone and the spirit of the town, and the painting pupils grew up and fell away and did not send their children to her with boxes of color and tedious brushes and pictures cut from the ladies' magazines. The front door closed upon the last one and remained closed for good. When the town got free postal delivery Miss Emily alone refused to let them fasten the metal numbers above her door and attach a mailbox to it. She would not listen to them.

Daily, monthly, yearly we watched the Negro grow grayer and more stooped, going in and out with the market basket. Each December we sent her a tax notice, which would be returned by the post office a week later, unclaimed. Now and then we would see her in one of the downstairs windows – she had evidently shut up the top floor of the house – like the carven torso of an idol in a niche, looking or not looking at us, we could never tell which. Thus she passed from generation to generation – dear, inescapable, impervious, tranquil, and perverse.

And so she died. Fell ill in the house filled with dust and shadows, with only a doddering Negro man to wait on her. We did not even know she was sick; we had long since given up trying to get any information from the Negro. He talked to no one, probably not even to her, for his voice had grown harsh and rusty, as if from disuse.

She died in one of the downstairs rooms, in a heavy walnut bed with a curtain, her gray head propped on a pillow yellow and moldy with age and lack of sunlight.

V

The Negro met the first of the ladies at the front door and let them in, with their hushed, sibilant° voices and their quick, curious glances, and then he disappeared. He walked right through the house and out the back and was not seen again.

The two female cousins came at once. They held the funeral on the second day, with the town coming to look at Miss Emily beneath a mass of bought flowers, with the crayon face of her father musing profoundly above the bier° and the ladies sibilant and macabre; and the very old men – some in their brushed Confederate uniforms – on the porch and the lawn, talking of Miss Emily as if she had been a contemporary of theirs, believing that they had danced with her and courted her perhaps, confusing time with its mathematical progression, as the old do, to whom all the past is not a diminishing road, but, instead, a huge meadow which no winter ever quite touches, divided from them now by the narrow bottleneck of the most recent decade of years.

Already we knew that there was one room in that region above stairs which no one had seen in forty years, and which would have to be forced. They waited until Miss Emily was decently in the ground before they opened it.

The violence of breaking down the door seemed to fill this room with pervading dust. A thin, acrid pall* as of the tomb seemed to lie everywhere upon this room decked and furnished as for a bridal: upon the valance* curtains of faded rose color, upon the rose-shaded lights, upon the dressing table, upon the delicate array of crystal and the man's toilet things backed with tarnished silver, silver so tarnished that the monogram was obscured. Among them lay a collar and tie, as if they had just been removed, which, lifted, left upon the surface a pale crescent in the dust. Upon a chair hung the suit, carefully folded; beneath it the two mute shoes and the discarded socks.

The man himself lay in the bed.

For a long while we just stood there, looking down at the profound and fleshless grin. The body had apparently once lain in the attitude of an embrace, but now the long sleep that outlasts love, that conquers even the grimace of love, had cuckolded* him. What was left of him, rotted beneath what was left of the nightshirt, had become inextricable from the bed in which he lay; and upon him and upon the pillow beside him lay that even coating of the patient and biding dust.

Then we noticed that in the second pillow was the indentation of a head. One of us lifted something from it, and leaning forward, that faint and invisible dust dry and acrid in the nostrils, we saw a long strand of iron-gray hair.

Thief

Robley Wilson Jnr

He is waiting at the airline ticket counter when he first notices the young woman. She has glossy black hair pulled tightly into a knot at the back of her head – the man imagines it loosed and cascading to the small of her back – and carries over the shoulder of her leather coat a heavy black purse. She wears black boots of soft leather. He struggles to see her face – she is ahead of him in line – but it is not until she has bought her ticket and turns to walk away that he realizes her beauty, which is pale and dark-eyed and full-mouthed, and which quickens his heartbeat. She seems aware that he is staring at her and lowers her gaze abruptly.

The airline clerk interrupts. The man gives up looking at the woman – he thinks she may be about twenty-five – and buys a round-trip, coach class ticket to an eastern city.

His flight leaves in an hour. To kill time, the man steps into one of the airport cocktail bars and orders a scotch and water. While he sips it he watches the flow of travelers through the terminal – including a remarkable number, he thinks, of unattached pretty women dressed in fashion magazine clothes – until he catches sight of the black-haired girl in the leather coat. She is standing near a Travelers Aid counter, deep in conversation with a second girl, a blonde in a cloth coat trimmed with gray fur. He wants somehow to attract the brunette's attention, to invite her to have a drink with him before her own flight leaves for wherever she is traveling, but even though he believes for a moment she is looking his way he cannot catch her eye from out of the shadows of the bar. In another instant the two women separate; neither of their directions is toward him. He orders a second scotch and water.

When next he sees her, he is buying a magazine to read during the flight and becomes aware that someone is jostling him. At first he is startled that anyone would be so close as to touch him, but when he sees who it is he musters a smile.

'Busy place,' he says.

She looks up at him – Is she blushing? – and an odd grimace crosses her mouth and vanishes. She moves away from him and joins the crowds in the terminal.

The man is at the counter with his magazine, but when he reaches into his back pocket for his wallet the pocket is empty. *Where could I have lost it?* he thinks. His mind begins enumerating the credit cards, the currency, the membership and identification cards; his stomach churns with something very like fear. *The girl who was so near to me*, he thinks – and all at once he understands that she has picked his pocket.

What is he to do? He still has his ticket, safely tucked inside his suitcoat – he reaches into the jacket to feel the envelope, to make sure. He can take the flight, call someone to pick him up at his destination – since he cannot even afford the bus fare – conduct his business and fly home. But in the meantime he will have to do something about the lost credit cards – call home, have his wife get the numbers out of the top desk drawer, phone the card companies – so difficult a process, the whole thing suffocating. What shall he do?

First: Find a policeman, tell what has happened, describe the young woman; damn her, he thinks, for seeming to be attentive to him, to let herself stand so close to him, to blush prettily when he spoke – and all the time she wanted only to steal from him. And her blush was not shyness but the anxiety of being caught; that was most disturbing of all. *Damned deceitful creatures*. He will spare the policeman the details – just tell what she has done, what is in the wallet. He grits his teeth. He will probably never see his wallet again.

He is trying to decide if he should save time by talking to a guard near the x-ray machines when he is appalled – and elated – to see the black-haired girl. (*Ebony-Tressed*° *Thief*, the newspapers will say.) She is seated against a front window of the terminal, taxis and private cars moving sluggishly beyond her in the gathering darkness; she seems engrossed in a book. A seat beside her is empty, and the man occupies it.

'I've been looking for you,' he says.

She glances at him with no sort of recognition. 'I don't know you,' she says.

'Sure you do.'

She sighs and puts the book aside. 'Is this all you characters think about – picking up girls like we were stray animals? What do you think I am?'

'You lifted my wallet,' he says. He is pleased to have said 'lifted,' thinking it sounds more worldly than *stole* or *took* or even *ripped off*.

'I beg your pardon?' the girl says.

'I know you did – at the magazine counter. If you'll just give it back, we can forget the whole thing. If you don't, then I'll hand you over to the police.'

She studies him, her face serious. 'All right,' she says. She pulls the black bag onto her lap, reaches into it and draws out a wallet.

He takes it from her. 'Wait a minute,' he says. 'This isn't mine.'

The girl runs; he bolts after her. It is like a scene in a movie – bystanders scattering, the girl zig-zagging to avoid collisions, the sound of his own breathing reminding him how old he is – until he hears a woman's voice behind him:

'Stop, thief! Stop that man!'

Ahead of him the brunette disappears around a corner and in the same moment a young man in a marine uniform puts out a foot to trip him up. He falls hard, banging knee and elbow on the tile floor of the terminal, but manages to hang on to the wallet which is not his.

The wallet is a woman's, fat with money and credit cards from places like Sak's and Peck & Peck and Lord & Taylor,° and it belongs to the blonde in the fur-trimmed coat – the blonde he has earlier seen in conversation with the criminal brunette. She, too, is breathless, as is the policeman with her.

'That's him,' the blonde girl says. 'He lifted my billfold.'

It occurs to the man that he cannot even prove his own identity to the policeman.

Two weeks later – the embarrassment and rage have diminished, the family lawyer has been paid, the confusion in his household has receded – the wallet turns up without explanation in one morning's mail. It is intact, no money is missing, all the cards are in place. Though he is relieved, the man thinks that for the rest of his life he will feel guilty around policemen, and ashamed in the presence of women.

The July Ghost

A. S. Byatt

'I think I must move out of where I'm living,' he said. 'I have this problem with my landlady.'

He picked a long, bright hair off the back of her dress, so deftly that the act seemed simply considerate. He had been skilful at balancing glass, plate and cutlery, too. He had a look of dignified misery, like a dejected hawk. She was interested.

'What sort of problem? Amatory, financial, or domestic?'

'None of those, really. Well, not financial.'

He turned the hair on his finger, examining it intently, not meeting her eye.

'Not financial. Can you tell me? I might know somewhere you could stay. I know a lot of people.'

'You would.' He smiled shyly. 'It's not an easy problem to describe. There's just the two of us. I occupy the attics. Mostly.'

He came to a stop. He was obviously reserved and secretive. But he was telling her something. This is usually attractive.

'Mostly?' Encouraging him.

'Oh, it's not like *that*. Well, not … Shall we sit down?'

They moved across the party, which was a big party, on a hot day. He stopped and found a bottle and filled her glass. He had not needed to ask what she was drinking. They sat side by side on a sofa: he admired the brilliant poppies bold on her emerald dress, and her pretty sandals. She had come to London for the summer to work in the British Museum. She could really have managed with microfilm in Tucson for what little manuscript research was needed, but there was a dragging love affair to end. There is an age at which, however desperately happy one is in stolen moments, days, or weekends with one's married professor, one either prises him loose or cuts and runs. She had had a stab at both, and now considered she had successfully cut and run. So it was nice to be immediately appreciated. Problems are capable of solution. She said as much to him, turning her soft face to his ravaged one, swinging the long bright hair. It had begun a year ago, he told her in a rush, at another party actually; he had met this woman, the landlady in question, and had made, not immediately, a kind of *faux pas*,⬦ he now saw, and she had been very decent, all things considered, and so ...

He had said, 'I think I must move out of where I'm living.' He had been quite wild, had nearly not come to the party, but could not go on drinking alone. The woman had considered him coolly and asked, 'Why?' One could not, he said, go on in a place where one had once been blissfully happy, and was now miserable, however convenient the place. Convenient, that was, for work, and friends, and things that seemed, as he mentioned them, ashy and insubstantial compared to the memory and the hope of opening the door and finding Anne outside it, laughing and breathless, waiting to be told what he had read, or thought, or eaten, or felt that day. Someone I loved left, he told the woman. Reticent on that occasion too, he bit back the flurry of sentences about the total unexpectedness of it, the arriving back and finding only an envelope on a clean table, and spaces in the bookshelves, the record stack, the kitchen cupboard. It must have been planned for weeks, she must have been thinking it out while he rolled on her, while she poured wine for him, while ... No, no. Vituperation⬦ is undignified and in this case what he felt was lower and worse than rage: just pure, child-like loss. 'One ought not to mind places,' he said to the woman. 'But one does,' she had said. 'I know.'

She had suggested to him that he could come and be her lodger, then; she had, she said, a lot of spare space going to waste, and her husband wasn't there much. 'We've not had a lot to say to each other, lately.' He could be quite self-contained, there was a kitchen and a bathroom in the attics; she wouldn't bother him. There was a large garden. It was possibly this that decided him: it was very hot, central London, the time of year when a man feels he would give anything to live in a room opening on to grass and trees, not a high flat in a dusty street. And if Anne came back, the door would be locked and mortice-locked.* He could stop thinking about Anne coming back. That was a decisive move: Anne thought he wasn't decisive. He would live without Anne.

For some weeks after he moved in he had seen very little of the woman. They met on the stairs, and once she came up, on a hot Sunday, to tell him he must feel free to use the garden. He had offered to do some weeding and mowing and she had accepted. That was the weekend her husband came back, driving furiously up to the front door, running in, and calling in the empty hall, 'Imogen, Imogen!' To which she had replied, uncharacteristically, by screaming hysterically. There was nothing in her husband, Noel's, appearance to warrant this reaction; their lodger, peering over the banister at the sound, had seen their upturned faces in the stairwell and watched hers settle into its usual prim and placid expression as he did so. Seeing Noel, a balding, fluffy-templed, stooping thirty-five or so, shabby corduroy suit, cotton polo neck, he realized he was now able to guess her age, as he had not been. She was a very neat woman, faded blonde, her hair in a knot on the back of her head, her legs long and slender, her eyes downcast. Mild was not quite the right word for her, though. She explained then that she had screamed because Noel had come home unexpectedly and startled her: she was sorry. It seemed a reasonable explanation. The extraordinary vehemence of the screaming was probably an echo in the stairwell. Noel seemed wholly downcast by it, all the same.

He had kept out of the way, that weekend, taking the stairs two at a time and lightly, feeling a little aggrieved, looking out of his kitchen window into the lovely, overgrown garden, that they were lurking indoors, wasting all the summer sun. At Sunday lunch-time he had heard the husband, Noel, shouting on the stairs.

'I can't go on, if you go on like that. I've done my best, I've tried to get through. Nothing will shift you, will it, you won't *try*, will you, you just go on and on. Well, I have my life to live, you can't throw a life away … can you?'

He had crept out again on to the dark upper landing and seen her standing, half-way down the stairs, quite still, watching Noel wave his arms and roar, or almost roar, with a look of impassive patience, as though this nuisance must pass off. Noel swallowed and gasped; he turned his face up to her and said plaintively,

'You do see I can't stand it? I'll be in touch, shall I? You must want … you must need … you must …

She didn't speak.

'If you need anything, you know where to get me.'

'Yes.'

'Oh, well … ' said Noel, and went to the door. She watched him, from the stairs, until it was shut, and then came up again, step by step, as though it was an effort, a little, and went on coming, past her bedroom, to his landing, to come in and ask him, entirely naturally, please to use the garden if he wanted to, and please not to mind marital rows. She was sure he understood … things were difficult … Noel wouldn't be back for some time. He was a journalist: his work took him away a lot. Just as well. She committed herself to that 'just as well'. She was a very economical speaker.

So he took to sitting in the garden. It was a lovely place: a huge, hidden, walled south London garden, with old fruit trees at the end, a wildly waving disorderly buddleia, curving beds full of old roses, and a lawn of overgrown, dense rye-grass. Over the wall at the foot was the Common, with a footpath running behind all the gardens. She came out to the shed and helped him to assemble and oil the lawnmower, standing on the little path under the apple branches while he cut an experimental serpentine across her hay. Over the wall came the high sound of children's voices, and the thunk and thud of a football. He asked her how to raise the blades: he was not mechanically minded.

'The children get quite noisy,' she said. 'And dogs. I hope they don't bother you. There aren't many safe places for children, round here.'

He replied truthfully that he never heard sounds that didn't concern him, when he was concentrating. When he'd got the lawn into shape, he was going to sit on it and do a lot of reading, try to get his mind in trim again, to write a paper on Hardy's° poems, on their curiously archaic vocabulary.

'It isn't very far to the road on the other side, really,' she said. 'It just seems to be. The Common is an illusion of space, really. Just a spur of brambles and gorse-bushes and bits of football pitch between two fast four-laned main roads. I hate London commons.'

'There's a lovely smell, though, from the gorse and the wet grass. It's a pleasant illusion.'

'No illusions are pleasant,' she said, decisively, and went in. He wondered what she did with her time: apart from little shopping expeditions she seemed to be always in the house. He was sure that when he'd met her she'd been introduced as having some profession: vaguely literary, vaguely academic, like everyone he knew. Perhaps she wrote poetry in her north-facing living-room. He had no idea what it would be like. Women generally wrote emotional poetry, much nicer than men, as Kingsley Amis° has stated, but she seemed, despite her placid stillness, too spare and too fierce – grim? – for that. He remembered the screaming. Perhaps she wrote Plath-like° chants of violence. He didn't think that quite fitted the bill, either. Perhaps she was a freelance radio journalist. He didn't bother to ask anyone who might be a common acquaintance. During the whole year, he explained to the American at the party, he hadn't actually *discussed* her with anyone. Of course he wouldn't, she agreed vaguely and warmly. She knew he wouldn't. He didn't see why he shouldn't, in fact, but went on, for the time, with his narrative.

They had got to know each other a little better over the next few weeks, at least on the level of borrowing tea, or even sharing pots of it. The weather had got hotter. He had found an old-fashioned deck-chair, with faded striped canvas, in the shed, and had brushed it over and brought it out on to his mown lawn, where he sat writing a little, reading a little, getting up and pulling up a tuft of couch grass. He had been wrong about the children not bothering him: there was a succession of incursions by all sizes of children looking for all sizes of balls, which bounced to his feet, or crashed in the shrubs, or vanished in the herbaceous border, black and white footballs, beach- balls with concentric circles of primary colours, acid yellow tennis balls. The children came over the wall: black faces, brown faces, floppy long hair, shaven heads, respectable dotted sun-hats and camouflaged cotton army hats from Milletts.° They came over easily, as though they were used to it, sandals, training shoes, a few bare toes, grubby sunburned legs, cotton skirts, jeans, football shorts. Sometimes, perched on the top, they saw him and gestured at the balls; one or two asked permission. Sometimes he threw a ball back, but was apt to knock down a few knobby little unripe apples or pears. There was a gate in the wall, under the fringing trees, which he once tried to open, spending time on rusty bolts only to discover that the lock was new and secure, and the key not in it.

The boy sitting in the tree did not seem to be looking for a ball. He was in a fork of the tree nearest the gate, swinging his legs, doing something to a knot in a frayed end of rope that was attached to the branch he sat on. He wore blue jeans and training shoes, and a brilliant tee shirt, striped in the colours of the spectrum, arranged in the right order, which the man on the grass found visually pleasing. He had rather long blond hair, falling over his eyes, so that his face was obscured.

'Hey, you. Do you think you ought to be up there? It might not be safe.'

The boy looked up, grinned, and vanished monkey-like over the wall. He had a nice, frank grin, friendly, not cheeky.

He was there again, the next day, leaning back in the crook of the tree, arms crossed. He had on the same shirt and jeans. The man watched him, expecting him to move again, but he sat, immobile, smiling down pleasantly, and then staring up at the sky. The man read a little, looked up, saw him still there, and said,

'Have you lost anything?'

The child did not reply: after a moment he climbed down a little, swung along the branch hand over hand, dropped to the ground, raised an arm in salute, and was up over the usual route over the wall.

Two days later he was lying on his stomach on the edge of the lawn, out of the shade, this time in a white tee shirt with a pattern of blue ships and water-lines on it, his bare feet and legs stretched in the sun. He was chewing a grass stem, and studying the earth, as though watching for insects. The man said, 'Hi, there,' and the boy looked up, met his look with intensely blue eyes under long lashes, smiled with the same complete warmth and openness, and returned his look to the earth.

He felt reluctant to inform on the boy, who seemed so harmless and considerate: but when he met him walking out of the kitchen door, spoke to him, and got no answer but the gentle smile before the boy ran off towards the wall, he wondered if he should speak to his landlady. So he asked her, did she mind the children coming in the garden. She said no, children must look for balls, that was part of being children. He persisted – they sat there, too, and he had met one coming out of the house. He hadn't seemed to be doing any harm, the boy, but you couldn't tell. He thought she should know.

He was probably a friend of her son's, she said. She looked at him kindly and explained. Her son had run off the Common with some other children, two years ago, in the summer, in July, and had been killed on the road. More or less instantly, she had added drily, as though calculating that just *enough* information would preclude the need for further questions. He said he was sorry, very sorry, feeling to blame, which was ridiculous, and a little injured, because he had not known about her son, and might inadvertently have made a fool of himself with some casual reference whose ignorance would be embarrassing.

What was the boy like, she said. The one in the house? 'I don't – talk to his friends. I find it painful. It could be Timmy, or Martin. They might have lost something, or want …'

He described the boy. Blond, about ten at a guess, he was not very good at children's ages, very blue eyes, slightly built, with a rainbow-striped tee shirt and blue jeans, mostly though not always – oh, and those football practice shoes, black and green. And the other tee shirt, with the ships and wavy lines. And an extraordinarily nice smile. A really *warm* smile. A nice-looking boy.

He was used to her being silent. But this silence went on and on and on. She was just staring into the garden. After a time, she said, in her precise conversational tone,

'The only thing I want, the only thing I want at all in this world, is to see that boy.'

She stared at the garden and he stared with her, until the grass began to dance with empty light, and the edges of the shrubbery wavered. For a brief moment he shared the strain of not seeing the boy. Then she gave a little sigh, sat down, neatly as always, and passed out at his feet.

After this she became, for her, voluble.° He didn't move her after she fainted, but sat patiently by her, until she stirred and sat up; then he fetched her some water, and would have gone away, but she talked.

'I'm too rational to see ghosts, I'm not someone who would see anything there was to see, I don't believe in an after-life, I don't see how anyone can, I always found a kind of satisfaction for myself in the idea that one just came to an end, to a sliced-off stop. But that was myself; I didn't think *he* – not *he* – I thought ghosts were – what people *wanted* to see, or were afraid to see … and after he died, the best hope I had, it sounds silly, was that I would go mad enough so that instead of waiting every day for him to come home from school and rattle the letter-box I might actually have the illusion of seeing or hearing him come in. Because I can't stop my body and mind waiting, every day, every day, I can't let go. And his bedroom, sometimes at night I go in, I think I might just for a moment forget he *wasn't* in there sleeping, I think I would pay almost anything – anything at all – for a moment of seeing him like I used to. In his pyjamas, with his – his – his hair … ruffled, and, his … you said, his … that *smile*.

'When it happened, they got Noel, and Noel came in and shouted my name, like he did the other day, that's why I screamed, because it – seemed the same – and then they said, he is dead, and I thought coolly, *is* dead, that will go on and on and on till the end of time, it's a continuous present tense, one thinks the most ridiculous things, there I was thinking about grammar, the verb to be, when it ends to be dead … And then I came out into the garden, and I half saw, in my mind's eye, a kind of ghost of his face, just the eyes and hair, coming towards me – like every day waiting for him to come home, the way you think of your son, with such pleasure, when he's – not there – and I – I thought – no, I won't *see* him, because he is dead, and I won't dream about him because he is dead, I'll be rational and practical and continue to live because one must, and there was Noel …

'I got it wrong, you see, I was so *sensible*, and then I was so shocked because I couldn't get to want anything – I couldn't *talk* to Noel – I – I – made Noel take away, destroy, all the photos, I – didn't dream, you can will not to dream, I didn't … visit a grave, flowers, there isn't any point. I was so sensible. Only my body wouldn't stop waiting and all it wants is to – to see that boy. *That* boy. That boy you – saw.'

He did not say that he might have seen another boy, maybe even a boy who had been given the tee shirts and jeans afterwards. He did not say, though the idea crossed his mind, that maybe what he had seen was some kind of impression from her terrible desire to see a boy where nothing was. The boy had had nothing terrible, no aura of pain about him: he had been, his memory insisted, such a pleasant, courteous, self-contained boy, with his own purposes. And in fact the woman herself almost immediately raised the possibility that what he had seen was what she desired to see, a kind of mix-up of radio waves, like when you overheard police messages on the radio, or got BBC I on a switch that said ITV. She was thinking fast, and went on almost immediately to say that perhaps his sense of loss, his loss of Anne, which was what had led her to feel she could bear his presence in her house, was what had brought them – dare she say – near enough, for their wavelengths to mingle, perhaps, had made him susceptible … You mean, he had said, we are a kind of emotional vacuum, between us, that must be filled. Something like that, she had said, and had added, 'But I don't believe in ghosts.'

Anne, he thought, could not be a ghost, because she was elsewhere, with someone else, doing for someone else those little things she had done so gaily for him, tasty little suppers, bits of research, a sudden vase of unusual flowers, a new bold shirt, unlike his own cautious taste, but suiting him, suiting him. In a sense, Anne was worse lost because voluntarily absent, an absence that could not be loved because love was at an end, for Anne.

'I don't suppose you will, now,' the woman was saying. 'I think talking would probably stop any – mixing of messages, if that's what it is, don't you? But – if – *if* he comes again' – and here for the first time her eyes were full of tears – 'if – you must promise, you will *tell* me, you must promise.'

He had promised, easily enough, because he was fairly sure she was right, the boy would not be seen again. But the next day he was on the lawn, nearer than ever, sitting on the grass beside the deck-chair, his arms clasping his bent, warm brown knees, the thick, pale hair glittering in the sun. He was wearing a football shirt, this time, Chelsea's colours. Sitting down in the deck-chair, the man could have put out a hand and touched him, but did not: it was not, it seemed, a possible gesture to make. But the boy looked up and smiled, with a pleasant complicity, as though they now understood each other very well. The man tried speech: he said, 'It's nice to see you again,' and the boy nodded acknowledgement of this remark, without speaking himself. This was the beginning of communication between them, or what the man supposed to be communication. He did not think of fetching the woman. He became aware that he was in some strange way *enjoying the boy's company.* His pleasant stillness – and he sat there all morning, occasionally lying back on the grass, occasionally staring thoughtfully at the house – was calming and comfortable. The man did quite a lot of work – wrote about three reasonable pages on Hardy's original air-blue gown˚ – and looked up now and then to make sure the boy was still there and happy.

He went to report to the woman – as he had after all promised to do – that evening. She had obviously been waiting and hoping – her unnatural calm had given way to agitated pacing, and her eyes were dark and deeper in. At this point in the story he found in himself a necessity to bowdlerize* for the sympathetic American, as he had indeed already begun to do. He had mentioned only a child who had 'seemed like' the woman's lost son, and he now ceased to mention the child at all, as an actor in the story, with the result that what the American woman heard was a tale of how he, the man, had become increasingly involved in the woman's solitary grief, how their two losses had become a kind of *folie à deux** from which he could not extricate himself. What follows is not what he told the American girl, though it may be clear at which points the bowdlerized version coincided with what he really believed to have happened. There was a sense he could not at first analyse that it was improper to talk about the boy – not because he might not be believed; that did not come into it; but because something dreadful might happen.

'He sat on the lawn all morning. In a football shirt.'

'Chelsea?'

'Chelsea.'

'What did he do? Does he look happy? Did he speak?' Her desire to know was terrible.

'He doesn't speak. He didn't move much. He seemed – very calm. He stayed a long time.'

'This is terrible. This is ludicrous. There *is no boy*.'

'No. But I saw him.'

'Why you?'

'I don't know.' A pause. 'I do *like* him.'

'He is – was – a most likeable boy.'

Some days later he saw the boy running along the landing in the evening, wearing what might have been pyjamas, in peacock towelling, or might have been a track suit. Pyjamas, the woman stated confidently, when he told her: his new pyjamas. With white ribbed cuffs, weren't they? and a white polo neck? He corroborated this, watching her cry – she cried more easily now – finding her anxiety and disturbance very hard to bear. But it never occurred to him that it was possible to break his promise to tell her when he saw the boy. That was another curious imperative from some undefined authority.

They discussed clothes. If there were ghosts, how could they appear in clothes long burned, or rotted, or worn away by other people? You could imagine, they agreed, that something of a person might linger – as the Tibetans and others believe the soul lingers near the body before setting out on its long journey. But clothes? And in this case so many clothes? I must be seeing your memories, he told her, and she nodded fiercely, compressing her lips, agreeing that this was likely, adding, 'I am too rational to go mad, so I seem to be putting it on you.'

He tried a joke. 'That isn't very kind to me, to imply that madness comes more easily to me.'

'No, sensitivity. I am insensible. I was always a bit like that, and this made it worse. I am the *last* person to see any ghost that was trying to haunt me.'

'We agreed it was your memories I saw.'

'Yes. We agreed. That's rational. As rational as we can be, considering.'

All the same, the brilliance of the boy's blue regard, his gravely smiling salutation in the garden next morning, did not seem like anyone's tortured memories of earlier happiness. The man spoke to him directly then:

'Is there anything I can *do* for you? Anything you want? Can I help you?'

The boy seemed to puzzle about this for a while, inclining his head as though hearing was difficult. Then he nodded, quickly and perhaps urgently, turned, and ran into the house, looking back to make sure he was followed. The man entered the living-room through the french windows, behind the running boy, who stopped for a moment in the centre of the room, with the man blinking behind him at the sudden transition from sunlight to comparative dark. The woman was sitting in an armchair, looking at nothing there. She often sat like that. She looked up, across the boy, at the man; and the boy, his face for the first time anxious, met the man's eyes again, asking, before he went out into the house.

'What is it? What is it? Have you seen him again? Why are you ...?'

'He came in here. He went – out through the door.'

'I didn't see him.'

'No.'

'Did he – oh, this is so *silly* – did he see me?'

He could not remember. He told the only truth he knew.

'He brought me in here.'

'Oh, what can I do, what am I going to *do*? If I killed myself – I have thought of that – but the idea that I should be with him is an illusion I ... this silly situation is the nearest I shall ever get. To him. He was *in here with me?*'

'Yes.'

And she was crying again. Out in the garden he could see the boy, swinging agile on the apple branch.

He was not quite sure, looking back, when he had thought he had realized what the boy had wanted him to do. This was also, at the party, his worst piece of what he called bowdlerization, though in some sense it was clearly the opposite of bowdlerization. He told the American girl that he had come to the conclusion that it was the woman herself who had wanted it, though there was in fact, throughout, no sign of her wanting anything except to see the boy, as she said. The boy, bolder and more frequent, had appeared several nights running on the landing, wandering in and out of bathrooms and bedrooms, restlessly, a little agitated, questing almost, until it had 'come to' the man that what he required was to be re-engendered, for him, the man, to give to his mother another child, into which he could peacefully vanish. The idea was so clear that it was like another imperative, though he did not have the courage to ask the child to confirm it. Possibly this was out of delicacy – the child was too young to be talked to about sex. Possibly there were other reasons. Possibly he was mistaken: the situation was making him hysterical, he felt action of some kind was required and must be possible. He could not spend the rest of the summer, the rest of his life, describing non-existent tee shirts and blond smiles.

He could think of no sensible way of embarking on his venture, so in the end simply walked into her bedroom one night. She was lying there, reading; when she saw him her instinctive gesture was to hide, not her bare arms and throat, but her book. She seemed, in fact, quite unsurprised to see his pyjamaed figure, and, after she had recovered her coolness, brought out the book definitely and laid it on the bedspread.

'My new taste in illegitimate literature. I keep them in a box under the bed.'

Ena Twig, Medium. The Infinite Hive. The Spirit World. Is There Life After Death?

'Pathetic,' she proffered.

He sat down delicately on the bed.

'Please, don't grieve so. Please, let yourself be comforted. Please ...'

He put an arm round her. She shuddered. He pulled her closer. He asked why she had had only the one son, and she seemed to understand the purport of his question, for she tried, angular and chilly, to lean on him a little, she became apparently compliant. 'No real reason,' she assured him, no material reason. Just her husband's profession and lack of inclination: that covered it.

'Perhaps,' he suggested, 'if she would be comforted a little, perhaps she could hope, perhaps …'

For comfort then, she said, dolefully, and lay back, pushing Ena Twigg off the bed with one fierce gesture, then lying placidly. He got in beside her, put his arms round her, kissed her cold cheek, thought of Anne, of what was never to be again. Come on, he said to the woman, you must live, you must try to live, let us hold each other for comfort.

She hissed at him 'Don't *talk*' between clenched teeth, so he stroked her lightly, over her nightdress, breasts and buttocks and long stiff legs, composed like an effigy° on an Elizabethan tomb. She allowed this, trembling slightly, and then trembling violently: he took this to be a sign of some mixture of pleasure and pain, of the return of life to stone. He put a hand between her legs and she moved them heavily apart; he heaved himself over her and pushed, unsuccessfully. She was contorted and locked tight: frigid, he thought grimly, was not the word. *Rigor mortis,*° his mind said to him, before she began to scream.

He was ridiculously cross about this. He jumped away and said quite rudely, 'Shut up,' and then ungraciously, 'I'm sorry.' She stopped screaming as suddenly as she had begun and made one of her painstaking economical explanations.

'Sex and death don't go. I can't afford to let go of my grip on myself. I hoped. What you hoped. It was a bad idea. I apologize.'

'Oh, never mind,' he said and rushed out again on to the landing, feeling foolish and almost in tears for warm, lovely Anne.

The child was on the landing, waiting. When the man saw him, he looked questioning, and then turned his face against the wall and leant there, rigid, his shoulders hunched, his hair hiding his expression. There was a similarity between woman and child. The man felt, for the first time, almost uncharitable towards the boy, and then felt something else.

'Look, I'm sorry. I tried. I did try. Please turn round.'

Uncompromising, rigid, clenched back view.

'Oh well,' said the man, and went into his bedroom.

So now, he said to the American woman at the party, I feel a fool, I feel embarrassed, I feel we are hurting, not helping each other, I feel it isn't a refuge. Of course you feel that, she said, of course you're right – it was temporarily necessary, it helped both of you, but you've got to live your life. Yes, he said, I've done my best, I've tried to get through, I have my life to live. Look, she said, I want to help, I really do, I have these wonderful friends I'm renting this flat from, why don't you come, just for a few days, just for a break, why don't you? They're real sympathetic people, you'd like them, I like them, you could get your emotions kind of straightened out. She'd probably be glad to see the back of you, she must feel as bad as you do, she's got to relate to her situation in her own way in the end. We all have.

He said he would think about it. He knew he had elected to tell the sympathetic American because he had sensed she would be – would offer – a way out. He had to get out. He took her home from the party and went back to his house and landlady without seeing her into her flat. They both knew that this reticence was promising – that he hadn't come in then, because he meant to come later. Her warmth and readiness were like sunshine, she was open. He did not know what to say to the woman.

In fact, she made it easy for him: she asked, briskly, if he now found it perhaps uncomfortable to stay, and he replied that he had felt he should move on, he was of so little use … Very well, she had agreed, and had added crisply that it had to be better for everyone if 'all this' came to an end. He remembered the firmness with which she had told him that no illusions were pleasant. She was strong: too strong for her own good. It would take years to wear away that stony, closed, simply surviving insensibility. It was not his job. He would go. All the same, he felt bad.

He got out his suitcases and put some things in them. He went down to the garden, nervously, and put away the deck-chair. The garden was empty. There were no voices over the wall. The silence was thick and deadening. He wondered, knowing he would not see the boy again, if anyone else would do so, or if, now he was gone, no one would describe a tee shirt, a sandal, a smile, seen, remembered, or desired. He went slowly up to his room again.

The boy was sitting on his suitcase, arms crossed, face frowning and serious. He held the man's look for a long moment, and then the man went and sat on his bed. The boy continued to sit. The man found himself speaking.

'You do see I have to go? I've tried to get through. I can't get through. I'm no use to you, am I?'

The boy remained immobile, his head on one side, considering. The man stood up and walked towards him.

'Please. Let me go. What are we, in this house? A man and a woman and a child, and none of us can get through. You can't want that?'

He went as close as he dared. He had, he thought, the intention of putting his hand on or through the child. But could not bring himself to feel there was no boy. So he stood, and repeated,

'I can't get through. Do you want me to stay?'

Upon which, as he stood helplessly there, the boy turned on him again the brilliant, open, confiding, beautiful desired smile.

The Waste Land

Alan Paton

The moment that the bus moved on he knew he was in danger, for by the lights of it he saw the figures of the young men waiting under the tree. That was the thing feared by all, to be waited for by the young men. It was a thing he had talked about, now he was to see it for himself.

It was too late to run after the bus; it went down the dark street like an island of safety in a sea of perils. Though he had known of his danger only for a second, his mouth was already dry, his heart was pounding in his breast, something within him was crying out in protest against the coming event.

His wages were in his purse, he could feel them weighing heavily against his thigh. That was what they wanted from him. Nothing counted against that. His wife could be made a widow, his children made fatherless, nothing counted against that. Mercy was the unknown word.

While he stood there irresolute he heard the young men walking towards him, not only from the side where he had seen them, but from the other also. They did not speak, their intention was unspeakable. The sound of their feet came on the wind to him. The place was well chosen, for behind him was the high wall of the convent, and the barred door that would not open before a man was dead. On the other side of the road was the waste land, full of wire and iron and the bodies of old cars. It was his only hope, and he moved towards it; as he did so he knew from the whistle that the young men were there too.

His fear was great and instant, and the smell of it went from his body to his nostrils. At that very moment one of them spoke, giving directions. So trapped was he that he was filled suddenly with strength and anger, and he ran towards the waste land swinging his heavy stick. In the darkness a form loomed up at him, and he swung the stick at it, and heard it give a cry of pain. Then he plunged blindly into the wilderness of wire and iron and the bodies of old cars.

Something caught him by the leg, and he brought his stick crashing down on it, but it was no man, only some knife-edged piece of iron. He was sobbing and out of breath, but he pushed on into the waste, while behind him they pushed on also, knocking against the old iron bodies and kicking against tins and buckets. He fell into some grotesque shape of wire; it was barbed and tore at his clothes and flesh. Then it held him, so that it seemed to him that death must be near, and having no other hope, he cried out, 'Help me, help me!' in what should have been a great voice but was voiceless and gasping. He tore at the wire, and it tore at him too, ripping his face and his hands.

Then suddenly he was free. He saw the bus returning, and he cried out again in the great voiceless voice, 'Help me, help me!' Against the lights of it he could plainly see the form of one of the young men. Death was near him, and for a moment he was filled with the injustice of life, that could end thus for one who had always been hardworking and law-abiding. He lifted the heavy stick and brought it down on the head of his pursuer, so that the man crumpled to the ground, moaning and groaning as though life had been unjust to him also.

Then he turned and began to run again, but ran first into the side of an old lorry which sent him reeling. He lay there for a moment expecting the blow that would end him, but even then his wits came back to him, and he turned over twice and was under the lorry. His very entrails seemed to be coming into his mouth, and his lips could taste sweat and blood. His heart was like a wild thing in his breast, and seemed to lift his whole body each time that it beat. He tried to calm it down, thinking it might be heard, and tried to control the noise of his gasping breath, but he could not do either of these things.

Then suddenly against the dark sky he saw two of the young men. He thought they must hear him; but they themselves were gasping like drowned men, and their speech came by fits and starts.

Then one of them said, 'Do you hear?'

They were silent except for their gasping, listening. And he listened also, but could hear nothing but his own exhausted heart.

'I heard a man ... running ... on the road,' said one. 'He's got away ... let's go.'

Then some more of the young men came up, gasping and cursing the man who had got away.

'Freddy,' said one, 'your father's got away.'

But there was no reply.

'Where's Freddy?' one asked.

One said, 'Quiet!' Then he called in a loud voice, 'Freddy.'

But still there was no reply.

'Let's go,' he said.

They moved off slowly and carefully, then one of them stopped.

'We are saved,' he said. 'Here is the man.'

He knelt down on the ground, and then fell to cursing.

'There's no money here,' he said.

One of them lit a match, and in the small light of it the man under the lorry saw him fall back.

'It's Freddy,' one said. 'He's dead.'

Then the one who had said 'Quiet' spoke again.

'Lift him up,' he said. 'Put him under the lorry.'

The man under the lorry heard them struggling with the body of the dead young man, and he turned once, twice, deeper into his hiding-place. The young men lifted the body and swung it under the lorry so that it touched him. Then he heard them moving away, not speaking, slowly and quietly, making an occasional sound against some obstruction in the waste.

He turned on his side, so that he would not need to touch the body of the young man. He buried his face in his arms, and said to himself in the idiom of his own language, 'People, arise! The world is dead.' Then he arose himself, and went heavily out of the waste land.

The Terrible Screaming

Janet Frame

One night a terrible screaming sounded through the city. It sounded so loudly and piercingly that there was not a soul who did not hear it. Yet when people turned to one another in fear and were about to remark, Did you hear it, that terrible screaming? they changed their minds, thinking, Perhaps it was my imagination, perhaps I have been working too hard or letting my thoughts get the upper hand (one must never work too hard or be dominated by one's thoughts), perhaps if I confess that I heard this terrible screaming others will label me insane, I shall be hidden behind locked doors and sit for the remaining years of my life in a small corner, gazing at the senseless writing on the wall.

Therefore no one confessed to having heard the screaming. Work and play, love and death, continued as usual. Yet the screaming persisted. It sounded day and night in the ears of the people of the city, yet all remained silent concerning it, and talked of other things. Until one day a stranger arrived from a foreign shore. As soon as he arrived in the city he gave a start of horror and exclaimed to the Head of the Welcoming Committee, 'What was that? Why, it has not yet ceased! What is it, that terrible screaming? How can you possibly live with it? Does it continue day and night? Oh what sympathy I have for you in this otherwise fair untroubled city!'

The Head of the Welcoming Committee was at a loss. On the one hand the stranger was a Distinguished Person whom it would be impolite to contradict; on the other hand, it would be equally unwise for the Head of the Welcoming Committee to acknowledge the terrible screaming. He decided to risk being thought impolite.

'I hear nothing unusual,' he said lightly, trying to suggest that perhaps his thoughts had been elsewhere, and at the same time trying to convey his undivided attention to the concern of the Distinguished Stranger. His task was difficult. The packaging of words with varied intentions is like writing a letter to someone in a foreign land and addressing it to oneself; it never reaches its destination.

The Distinguished Stranger looked confused. 'You hear no terrible screaming?'

The Head of the Welcoming Committee turned to his assistant. 'Do you perhaps hear some unusual sound?'

The Assistant who had been disturbed by the screaming and had decided that very day to speak out, to refuse to ignore it, now became afraid that perhaps he would lose his job if he mentioned it. He shook his head.

'I hear nothing unusual,' he replied firmly.

The Distinguished Stranger looked embarrassed. 'Perhaps it is my imagination,' he said apologetically. 'It is just as well that I have come for a holiday to your beautiful city. I have been working very hard lately.'

Then aware once again of the terrible screaming he covered his ears with his hands.

'I fear I am unwell,' he said. 'I apologise if I am unable to attend the banquet, in honour of my arrival.'

'We understand completely,' said the Head of the Welcoming Committee.

So there was no banquet. The Distinguished Stranger consulted a specialist who admitted him to a private rest home where he could recover from his disturbed state of mind and the persistence in his ears of the terrible screaming.

The Specialist finished examining the Distinguished Stranger. He washed his hands with a slab of hard soap, took off his white coat, and was preparing to go home to his wife when he thought suddenly, Suppose the screaming does exist?

He dismissed the thought. The Rest Home was full, and the fees were high. He enjoyed the comforts of civilisation. Yet supposing, just supposing that all the patients united against him, that all the people of the city began to acknowledge the terrible screaming? What would be the result? Would there be complete panic? Was there really safety in numbers where ideas were concerned?

He stopped thinking about the terrible screaming. He climbed into his Jaguar and drove home.

The Head of the Welcoming Committee, disappointed that he could not attend another banquet, yet relieved because he would not be forced to justify another item of public expenditure, also went home to his wife. They dined on a boiled egg, bread and butter and a cup of tea, for they both approved of simple living.

Then he went to their bedroom, took off his striped suit, switched out the light, got into bed with his wife, and enjoyed the illusion of making uncomplicated love.

And outside in the city the terrible screaming continued its separate existence, unacknowledged. For you see its name was Silence. Silence had found its voice.

Dragons' Breath

A. S. Byatt

Once upon a time, in a village in a valley surrounded by high mountains, lived a family with two sons and a daughter, whose names were Harry, Jack and Eva. The village was on the lower slopes of the mountains, and in the deep bowl of the valley was a lake, clear as crystal on its shores, and black as ink in its unplumbed centre. Thick pine forests grew in the shadow of the mountain ridges, but the village stood amongst flowery meadows and orchards, and cornfields, not luscious, but sufficient for the needs of the villagers. The peaks of the mountains were inaccessible, with blue ice-shadows and glittering snow-fields. The sides of the mountain were scored with long descending channels, like the furrows of some monstrous plough. In England the circular impressions around certain hills are ascribed to the coiling grip of ancient dragons, and in that country there was a tale that in some primeval° time the channels had been cut by the descent of giant worms from the peaks. In the night, by the fire, parents frightened children pleasurably with tales of the flaming, cavorting descent of the dragons.

Harry, Jack and Eva were not afraid of dragons, but they were, in their different ways, afraid of boredom. Life in that village repeated itself, generation after generation. They were born, they became lovers, they became parents and grand-parents, they died. They were somewhat inbred, to tell the truth, for the outside world was far away, and hard to reach, and only a few traders came and went, in the summer months, irregularly. The villagers made a certain traditional kind of rug,

145

on handlooms, with a certain limited range of colours from vegetable dyes they made themselves – a blood-red, a dark blue with a hint of green, a sandy yellow, a charcoal black. There were a few traditional designs, which hardly varied: a branching tree, with fruit like pomegranates, and roosting birds, somewhat like pheasants, or a more abstract geometrical design, with discs of one colour threaded on a crisscrossing web of another on the ground of a third. The rugs were on the whole made by the women, who also cooked and washed. The men looked after the livestock, worked the fields and made music. They had their own musical instrument, a wailing pipe, not found anywhere else, though most of them had not travelled far enough to know that.

Harry was a swineherd and Jack dug in the fields, sowed and harvested. Harry had a particular friend amongst the pigs, a young boar called Boris, a sagacious° creature who made cunning escapes and dug up unexpected truffles.° But Boris's playfulness was not enough to mitigate Harry's prevailing boredom. He dreamed of great cities beyond the mountain, with streaming crowds of urgent people, all different, all busy. Jack liked to see the corn come up, green spikes in the black earth, and he knew where to find ceps° and wild honey, but these treats did little to mitigate his prevailing boredom. He dreamed of ornamental gardens inside high walls surrounding huge palaces. He dreamed of subtle tastes, spices and fiery spirits unknown in the valley. He dreamed also of wilder dances, bodies flung about freely, to music on instruments he knew only by hearsay: the zither, the bongo drum, the grand piano, tubular bells.

Eva made the rugs. She could have woven in her sleep, she thought, and often did, waking to find her mind buzzing with repeats and variations, twisting threads and shifting warp and weft. She dreamed of unknown colours, purple, vermilion,° turquoise and orange, colours of flowers and feathers, soft silks, sturdy cottons. She dreamed of an older Eva, robed in crimson and silver. She dreamed of the sea, which she could not imagine, she dreamed of salt water and tasted her own impatient tears. She was not good at weaving, she made her tension too tight, and her patterns bunched, but this was her task. She was a weaver. She wanted to be a traveller, a sailor, a learned doctor, an opera singer in front of flaring footlights and the roar of the crowd.

The first sign may have been the hunters' reports of unusual snow-slides in the high mountains. Or maybe it was, as some of them later claimed, dawns that were hectically rosy, sunsets that flared too crimson. They began to hear strange rumblings and crackings up there, above the snow-line, which they discussed, as they discussed every strange and every accustomed sound, with their repetitious measuring commentary that made Jack and Harry grind their teeth with rage at the sameness of it all. After a time it became quite clear that the rim of the mountains directly above the village, both by day and by night, was flickering and dancing with a kind of fiery haze, a smoky salmon-pink, a burst here and there of crimson and gold. The colours were rather beautiful, they agreed as they watched from their doorsteps, the bright ribbons of colour flashing through the grey-blue smokiness of the air, and then subsiding. Below this flaming rim the white of the snow was giving way to the gaunt grey of wet rock, and the shimmer – and yes, steam – of new water.

They must have been afraid from the beginning: they could see well enough that large changes were taking place, that everything was on the move, earth and air, fire and water. But the fear was mixed with a great deal of excited *interest*, and with even a certain pleasure in novelty, and with aesthetic pleasure, of which many of them were later ashamed. Hunting-parties went out in the direction of the phenomenon and came back to report that the hillside seemed to be on the move, and was boiling and burning, so that it was hard to see through the very thick clouds of ash and smoke and steam that hung over the movement. The mountains were not, as far as

anyone knew, volcanic, but the lives of men are short beside
the history of rocks and stones, so they wondered and debated.

After some time they saw on the skyline lumps like the
knuckles of a giant fist, six lumps, where nothing had been,
lumps that might represent objects the size of large sheds or
small houses, at that distance. And over the next few weeks the
lumps advanced, in smoke and spitting sparks, regularly and
slowly, side by side, without hesitation or deviation, down the
mountainside. Behind each tump⋄ trailed a long, unbending
tube, as it were, or furrow-ridge, or earth-work, coming over
the crest of the mountain, over the rim of their world, pouring
slowly on and down.

Some brave men went out to prospect but were forced back
by clouds of scalding steam and showers of burning grit. Two
friends, bold hunters both, went out and never returned.

One day a woman in her garden said: – 'It is almost as
though it was not landslides but creatures, great worms with
fat heads creeping down on us. Great fat, nodding bald heads,
with knobs and spouts and whelks and whorls⋄ on them, and
nasty hot wet eyes in great caverns in their muddy flesh, that
glint blood-red, twelve eyes, can you see them, and twelve hairy
nostrils on blunt snouts made of grey mud.' And after
conversations and comparisons and pointings and descriptions
they could all see them, and they were just as she said, six fat,
lolling, loathsome heads, trailing heavy bodies as long as the
road from their village to the next, trailing them with difficulty,
even with pain, it seemed, but unrelenting and deadly slow.

When they were nearer – and the slowness of their progress
was dreamlike, unreal – their great jaws could be seen, jaws
wide as whales and armed with a scythe-like horny or flinty
edge like a terrible beak, with which they excavated and
swallowed a layer of the earth and whatever was on it – bushes,
fences, haystacks, fruit trees, a couple of goats, a black and
white cow, a duckpond and the life in it. They sucked and
scythed, with a soughing noise, and they spat out fine ash, or

dribbled it from the lips of the terrible jaws, and it settled on everything. As they approached, the cloud of ash came before them, and settled on everything in the houses and gardens, coated the windows, filmed the wells. It stank, the ash, it was unspeakably foul. At first they grumbled and dusted, and then they gave up dusting, for it was no use, and began to be afraid. It was all so slow that there was a period of unreal, half-titillating fear, before the real, sick, paralysing fear took hold, which was when the creatures were close enough for men and women to see their eyes, which were rimmed with a gummy discharge, like melting rubber, and their tongues of flame. The tongues of flame were nothing like the brave red banners of painted dragons in churches, and nothing like the flaming swords of archangels. They were molten and lolling, covered with a leathery transparent skin thick with crimson warts and taste-buds glowing like coals, the size of cabbages, slavering with some sulphurous glue and stinking of despair and endless decay that would never be clean again in the whole life of the world. Their bodies were repulsive, as they humped and slithered and crushed, slow and grey and indiscriminate. Their faces were too big to be seen as faces – only identified in parts, successively. But the stench was the worst thing, and the stench induced fear, then panic, then a fatalistic tremor of paralysis, like rabbits before stoats, or mice before vipers.

The villagers discussed for far too long the chances of the village being destroyed. They discussed also expedients for diverting, or damaging the worms, but these were futile, and came to nothing. They discussed also the line of the creatures' advance; whether it crossed the village, or whether it might be projected to pass by it on one side or another. Afterwards it might have been easy to agree that it was always clear that the village stood squarely in the path of that terrible descent, but hope misleads, and inertia misleads, and it is hard to imagine the vanishing of what has seemed as stable as stone. So the villagers left it very late to make a plan to evacuate their village, and in the end left hurriedly and messily, running here and there in the stink and smoke of that bad breath, snatching up their belongings, putting them down and snatching up others, seething like an ants' nest. They ran into the forest with sacks of corn and cooking-pots, with feather-beds and sides of bacon, completely bewildered by the presence of the loathsome creatures. It was not clear that the worms exactly saw the human beings. The human beings were not on their scale, as small creatures that inhabit our scalps, or burrow in the salad leaves we eat are not visible to us, and we take no account of them.

The villagers' life in the forest became monotonous, boring even, since boredom is possible for human beings in patches of tedium between exertion and terror. They were very cold, especially at night, they were hungry and their stomachs were constantly queasy, both with fear and with their ramshackle diet. They knew they were beyond the perimeter of the worms' breath, and yet they smelt its foul odour, in their dreams, in the curl of smoke from their camp-fires, in rotting leaves. They had watchers posted, who were placed to be able to see in the distance the outline of the village, who saw the line of gross heads advancing imperceptibly, who saw bursts of sudden flame and spurts of dense smoke that must have been the kindling of houses. They were watching the destruction of their world, and yet they felt a kind of ennui◇ which was part of all the other distress they felt. You might ask – where were the knights, where were the warriors who would at least ride out and try to put an arrow or a bullet through those drooling eyes. There was talk of this round the camp-fires, but no heroes sprang up, and it is probable that this was wise, that the things were invulnerable to the pinprick of human weapons. The elders said it was best to let things go by, for those huge bodies would be almost as noisome◇ dead as alive in the village midst. The old women said that old tales told that dragons' breath paralysed the will, but when they were asked for practical advice, *now*, they had none to offer. You could want to kill yourself, Eva found out, because you were sleeping on a tree-root, on the hard ground, which pressed into your flesh and became an excruciating pain, boring in both senses.

Harry and Jack finally went with some other young men, out in the direction of the village, to see from close quarters the nature and extent of the devastation. They found they were walking towards a whole wall of evil-smelling smoke and flame, extending across acres of pastureland and cornfield, behind which the great crag-like protuberances of the heads could be seen, further apart now, moving on like the heads of water at the mouth of a flooding delta. Jack said to Harry that this fanning-out of the paths left little chance that anything in the village might be left standing, and Harry replied distractedly that there were figures of some sort moving in the smoke, and then said that they were the pigs, running here and there, squealing. A pig shot out of the smoke, panting and squeaking, and Harry called out, 'Boris!' and began to run after his pig, which snorted wildly and charged back into the darkness, followed by Harry, and Jack saw pig and human in sooty silhouette before he heard a monstrous sucking sound, and an exhalation of hot vapours and thick, choking fiery breath which sent him staggering and fainting back. When he came to, his skin was thick with adhesive ash and he could hear, it seemed to him, the liquids boiling and burning in the worm's belly.

For a moment he thought he would simply lie there, in the path of that jaw, and be scooped up with the cornfield and the hedgerow. Then he found he had decided to roll away, and little by little, rolling, crawling and scrambling, he put patches of space between himself and the worm. He lay for several hours, then, winded and sick, under a thornbush, before picking himself painfully up, and returning to the camp in the forest. He hoped that Harry too would return, but was not surprised, not really surprised, when he did not.

And so it dragged on, for weeks and months, with the air full of ash and falling cinders, with their clothes and flesh permeated by that terrible smell, until little by little the long loathsome bodies dragged past, across the fields and the meadows, leaving behind those same furrows of rocky surface, scooped clean of life and growth. And from a hilly point they saw the creatures, side by side, cross the sandy shore of the lake, and without changing pace or hesitating, advance across the shallows, as though driven by mechanical necessity, or by some organic need like the periodic return of toads or turtles to a watery world to breed. And the great heads dipped to meet the lake surface, and where they met it, it boiled, and steamed and spat like a great cauldron. And then the heads went under the surface, which still boiled, puckered and bubbling, as the slow lengths of the long bodies humped and slithered, day after day over the sand and down through the water to the depths, until finally only blunt, ugly butts could be seen, under the shallows, and then one day, as uncertainly as their coming had been established, it became clear that their going was over, that the worms had plunged into, through, under the lake, leaving only the harsh marks of their bodies' weight and burning breath in the soil, the rock, the vegetable world crushed and withered.

When the villagers returned to look on their village from a distance, the devastation seemed uniform: the houses flattened, the trees uprooted, the earth scored, channelled, ashy and smoking. They wandered in the ruins, turning over bricks and boards, some people finding, as some people always will, lost treasures and trivia in the ashes, a coin, half a book, a dented cooking-pot. And some people who had vanished in the early chaos returned, with singed eyebrows or seared faces, and others did not. Jack and Eva came back together, and for a moment could not work out in what direction to look for the ruins of what had been their house. And then, coming round a heap of fallen rubble they saw it there, untouched. One of the dragon-troughs passed at a distance, parallel to the garden fence, but the fence stood, and inside the fence the garden, the veranda, the doors and windows were as they had always been, apart from the drifting ash. And Jack lifted the stone under which the key was always kept, and there was the key, where it had always been. And Jack and Eva went into the house, and there were tables and chairs, fireplace and bookcase, and Eva's loom, standing in the window, at the back of the house, where you looked out on the slopes and then up at the peaks of the mountains. And there was a heavy humping sound against the back door, which Jack opened. And when he opened it, there was Boris the pig, hanging his head a little, and giving off an odour of roast pork, with not a bristle on his charred rind, but with pleasure and recognition in his deepset little eyes.

When they saw that the pig had by some miracle, or kindness of luck, escaped the dragon-breath and the fiery tongues, they hoped, of course, that Harry too would return. They hoped he would return for days and months, and against their reasonable judgment, for years. But he did not.

Eva dusted her rug, which was lightly filmed with ash, since it was at the back of the house, and the windows were well-made. She saw the colours – red, blue, yellow, black – as though she had never seen colour before, and yet with disturbed pleasure at their familiarity. An archaeologist, finding this room, and this rug on this loom in it, say two thousand years later, might have felt intense excitement that these things were improbably intact, and intense curiosity about the workmanship, and about the even daily life that could be partly imagined around the found artefacts. Eva felt such amazement now, about her own work, the stubborn persistence of wood and wool and bone shuttle, or the unfinished tree with its squatting pheasants and fat pomegranates. She felt inwardly moved and shaken, also, by this form of her own past, and the past of her mother and grandmother, and by the traces of her moments of flowing competence, and of her periods of bunching, tension, anxiety, fumbling. Jack too felt delight and amazement, walking repeatedly across the house from the windows which opened on smouldering devastation to those from which you could see the unchanging mountains. Both embraced Boris, restored and rescued, feeling his wet snout and warm flanks. Such wonder, such amazement, are the opposite, the exact opposite, of boredom, and many people only know them after fear and loss. Once known, I believe, they cannot be completely forgotten; they cast flashes and floods of paradisal light⋄ in odd places and at odd times.

The villagers rebuilt their village, and the rescued things in the rescued house stood amongst new houses in whose gardens new flowers and vegetables sprouted, and new saplings were planted. The people began to tell tales about the coming of the worms down the mountain, and the tales too were the opposite of boredom. They made ash and bad breath, crushing and swallowing, interesting, exciting, almost beautiful. Some things they made into tales, and some things they did not speak. Jack told of Harry's impetuous bravery, rushing into the billowing smoke to save his pig, and nobody told the day-to-day misery of the slowly diminishing hope of his return. The resourcefulness and restoration of the pig were celebrated, but not his inevitable fate, in these hard days. And these tales, made from those people's wonder at their own survival, became in time, charms against boredom for their children and grandchildren, riddling hints of the true relations between peace and beauty and terror.

RESOURCE NOTES

Who has written these short stories and why?

Uses and abuses of the lives of writers

The act of reading is never straightforward. One view of reading suggests that when you read you are using one text to interpret another, even if one of those texts is inside your own head. So, for example, if you read a modern fairy tale you are using your knowledge of the original to guide you. If the modern writer creates a Red Riding Hood with intelligence and strength, your knowledge of the original tells you that the writer is probably making a point about the roles of women in society. Sometimes you read a story with another text literally alongside it, to explicitly guide your reading – as in the case of these notes. However, some texts are more powerful than others, and a particularly appealing and powerful text is the life story of the writer in question. It is very tempting to assume that a story can be explained by knowing about the writer's life. Biographical information should not replace our own response but rather enhance it.

Why short stories?

Submerged population groups

Do the writers in this collection have something in common because they all write short stories? A starting point could be the work of Frank O'Connor (1903–1966). O'Connor believed that short story writers tend to come from 'submerged population groups' distinct from the national community as a whole. He had in mind oppressed nations such as the Irish or, more recently, Afro-Caribbean writers living in Britain. The idea can also be extended outside national identity to other social groups, the most obvious one being women: many of the great short story writers have been women – Katherine

Mansfield (a New Zealander who lived in Britain), Elizabeth Bowen, Nadine Gordimer, Carson McCullers. O'Connor's theory also extends to the content of the stories themselves – which tend to be about outsiders (see page 170).

✦ *Activity*

Read the following accounts of writers' lives. On this evidence do you agree with O'Connor's theory about the writers of short stories? You may, of course, wish to do some further research into their lives, using a school or public library.

Raymond Carver (1938–1988)

In his collection *Fires*, which was published shortly before his death in 1988, Carver said he had trouble concentrating on both the reading and the writing of long fiction. He had little time for literary influences:

> I have to say that the greatest influence on my life and writing, directly and indirectly, has been my two children … there wasn't any area of my life where their heavy and often baleful influence didn't reach … My life was a small-change thing for the most part, chaotic, with little light showing through.
>
> (*The Sunday Times*, January 1995)

The titles of the stories in *Fires* perhaps reveal something of that chaos: 'Drinking while Driving'; 'Bankruptcy'; 'Alcohol'; 'Looking for Work'; 'Where is Everyone?' Although Carver was happy in his final years – he called them 'pure gravy' – his stories are known for their sense of 'dis-ease'.

Two films of Carver's stories have recently been made: *Short Cuts*, directed by Robert Altman (1993) combines ten short stories into a single narrative. *Tropical Fish*, directed by British writer/director Chris Rodley (1994) is an adaptation of a story about a dull couple who are asked by their neighbours to look after their fish tank while they are away.

Janet Frame (1924–)

Janet Frame was born into a poor family living on the South Island of New Zealand. Her childhood was marred by illness and the death of her brothers and sisters. At school she was extremely introverted and her ability to write poetry only emphasised her exclusion by others. After failing to qualify as a teacher she had a nervous breakdown and was incorrectly diagnosed as schizophrenic. She then suffered eight years of ill treatment at the hands of a mental institution before her first collection of short stories, *The Lagoon and Other Stories* (1951), convinced the authorities that she was in fact sane. She has since published several novels and collections of short stories. Frame's three-part autobiography, *An Angel at My Table* (1984) was made into a full-length film by Jane Campion in 1990.

Nikolai Gogol (1809–1852)

Born in the Ukraine, Nikolai Gogol went to St Petersburg in 1828 hoping for a literary career. He found life there dreary and depressing, complaining to his mother that:

> … all the civil servants can talk about is their government or department office; everything seems to have been crushed under a great weight, everyone is drowned by the trivial, meaningless labours at which he spends his useless life.
>
> (quoted in Ronald Wilks (trans.) *Diary of a Madman and other stories*, Penguin, 1972)

This was essentially a description of the rigid, highly impersonal, bureaucratic state machine of Nicholas the First's regime. This monarch had absolute power, and was considered the most severe of the Russian Tsars.

Gogol's short stories were at first escapist episodes about his homeland, the Ukraine. Later stories displayed a dreamlike blend of the sordid and the fantastic, often satirising the bureaucracy that surrounded him. Some critics have interpreted Gogol's stories as reflecting his own feelings of guilt and inadequacy, his anxieties and obsessions. He frequently creates very simple plots about exaggerated caricatures such as insignificant clerks or mere nobodies pretending to be government inspectors. His stories are critical of human pretension, often blurring the distinction between people and things.

When Gogol wrote 'Diary of a Madman' (which is set in St Petersburg) he was very interested in the idea of madness. He also wrote a censored play called *Vladimir Third Class* that dealt with this theme. It has been claimed that the 'Diary' blurs the divisions between illusion and reality and thus illustrates many of Gogol's own thwarted desires and obsessions. It also probably contains elements of his fear of sexual relations, his 'sterility complex'.

Charlotte Perkins Gilman (1860–1935)

Charlotte Perkins Gilman became one of America's most prominent feminist intellectuals, setting up her own feminist journal and writing non-fiction as well as fiction. Her childhood was lonely and without affection; she grew up unhappily, was married, and divorced in 1894 (an unusual event in those days). During her marriage she suffered a nervous breakdown from which she never fully recovered. It was during this period that she wrote 'The Yellow Wallpaper', the story for which she is best remembered. She committed suicide in 1935 whilst suffering from cancer.

William Boyd (1952–)

William Boyd was born in Ghana, but was educated at Gordonstoun School in Scotland. He has written several highly acclaimed novels including *The Blue Afternoon*, which won the *Sunday Express* Book of the Year award in 1993. Though he has sometimes been accused of offering a strong male perspective on the world, in two of his novels he has written from the point of view of a woman. Boyd himself commented: 'Nine years in a males only British public school took its toll.' He is a great story teller and often makes use of exotic locations which he presents with graphical accuracy. A common theme in his writing is order disrupted by the unexpected. He has also written two collections of short stories though some critics regard his novels as superior. One journalist (Stephen Amidon) wrote that his short stories were 'straightjacketed ... like Mike Tyson◊ throwing darts'. He has for several years written screenplays for Hollywood; he has adapted two of his novels for the screen and in Britain he has turned to broadcasting.

Robley Wilson Jnr (1930–)

Robley Wilson has written novels, poetry, literary criticism and history. He has been Professor of English at the University of North Iowa since 1975, having previously done a variety of jobs including that of newspaper reporter. His collection *Dancing for Men*, from which 'Thief' is taken, won an American literary award in 1983.

William Faulkner (1897–1962)

William Faulkner was one of the greatest of American writers. His major works were produced between 1929 and 1959 and he was best known for his novels that experimented with multiple points of view and captured the consciousness of his characters. In *The Sound and the Fury* (1929), for example, part of the story is told through the eyes of a thirty-year-old imbecile. As a child Faulkner grew up surrounded by local folk tales and this helped him to create his own fictional county which managed to capture a great deal of the spirit of the American South.◊ His work constantly returned to themes that explored obstacles to human freedom, such as prejudice, fear and pride. In 1949 he won the Nobel Prize for Literature.

Alan Paton (1903–1988)

Alan Paton is best known for his book *Cry The Beloved Country* (1948) which was one of the first books to expose the cruelty of the apartheid° regime in South Africa. He was born in Natal (now South Africa), educated in the sciences and became a teacher, eventually becoming principal of a reformatory for delinquent African boys near Johannesburg. He ran this on humanitarian principles, transforming it from a prison into a school, and this became the subject matter of much of his writing. He was National President of the Liberal Party in South Africa before it was disbanded in 1968, owing to pressure from the government. Much of his life was dedicated, somewhat reluctantly, to political activity.

Alice Munro (1931–)

Alice Munro was born in Ontario, Canada. She attended Western Ontario University and later opened a bookshop in Victoria. In 1972 she returned to the area of south-eastern Ontario where she grew up and where she now lives, at least for some of the time, with her second husband. As a writer she was a slow starter. Her first collection, *Dance of the Happy Shades*, appeared in 1968 and she didn't attract widespread attention until her second book, *Lives of Girls and Women*, which appealed to feminists, was published in 1971. She is one of the few writers to write almost exclusively short stories. Even her books that can claim to be novels, such as *Lives of Girls and Women*, are episodic and can also be regarded as linked stories. She has won several awards within Canada and has also been short-listed for the Booker Prize. Her most recent book, *Open Secrets* (1994), has been highly acclaimed by critics as a collection that experiments with the form of the short story in far more complex ways than her earlier work.

Susan Hill (1942–)

Susan Hill was born in Scarborough, England, and wrote her first novel, *The Enclosure* (1961), whilst still at school. She went on to write a series of novels, including *I'm the King of the Castle* (1970), in the late 1960s and early 1970s – all of which have been highly praised by critics. In her early twenties a relationship of eight years ended suddenly when her partner died. In 1975, she married an academic who specialises in the study of Shakespeare, gave birth to a daughter in 1977, but her second child died at five weeks old in 1984. After great difficulties she gave birth to another daughter in 1985 and she has since written a book, *Family* (1989), about her determination to be a mother again. In the mid-1980s she announced that she did not intend to write any more novels, but then in 1993 she wrote a sequel to Daphne du Maurier's *Rebecca* (1938) entitled *Mrs de Winter*.

A. S. Byatt (1936–)

Antonia Byatt was born into a brilliant family that also included her sister, the author Margaret Drabble. Byatt has written many novels and several collections of short stories, many of which bear the stamp of someone who is an academic as well as a writer. In the early years Byatt was over-shadowed by her younger sister's early success, and then in the 1970s she suffered a creative drought largely due to personal circumstances. It was at this time that her eleven-year-old son was tragically killed in a car accident. Her 1990 novel, *Possession*, which won the Booker Prize, changed her from an interesting minor writer into an international celebrity.

Byatt has written that, 'The stories of women's lives in fiction are the story of stopped energies.' You might consider how far this applies to the woman in 'The July Ghost'.

✦ *Activities*

1 You have been asked to contribute to a series of five-minute radio programmes about the lives of famous writers. One programme is to be dedicated to short story writers. Choose

two or three authors from the above list and write the script for your programme, bearing in mind the following:

- how you will make links between the writers you choose;
- which short extracts from the stories you will use to illustrate the authors' work;
- how you will make use of the above biographies and the notes on how these stories were produced on pages 163–168;
- how you will structure and vary the content in order to interest and entertain your audience.

2 Susan Hill believes that all novelists are compensating for something that is missing in their lives. To what extent do you believe that this is also true of the writers in this collection? Discuss this with a partner, making a list of the feelings the writer might be expressing in each story and then check this against the biographical notes presented in this section.

◆

How were these short stories produced?

Gathering ideas

Writers often begin their careers with short story writing. They know that they want to write prose rather than poetry, and short stories are a convenient place to start. But where do writers, or potential writers, get their ideas from? The most obvious answer is from life, but this, on its own, tells us very little. 'Life' may provide a feeling to be expressed (as in 'The July Ghost'), the setting (as in the work of Alice Munro and William Boyd), the basic 'stuff' or context from which the story is eventually shaped (as in Alan Paton and Raymond Carver), or a particular philosophy to be pursued (as in Charlotte Perkins Gilman). But writers don't always have the choice. The personal tragedy of the death of A. S. Byatt's son in a car accident clearly left her with feelings to be worked out many years later. The following poem appeared in *The Times Literary Supplement* in 1994:

> Our son is many sons
> A bundle, a putto,° a grave
> Boy with kind eyes. One blow
> Cracks all their bones at once.
> Plasters all the gold hair red ...

This fragment and 'The July Ghost' show that writers shape their feelings so that the same idea may be expressed in a number of different ways. But individual writers use different methods; it's a case of using whatever method works best for you. Some writers begin with an emotion they have experienced in real life and then transform it to another situation by asking the question 'What if ... this happened?' Others start with a 'theme'. Frank O'Connor (see page 155) describes one of the problems he faced in teaching writing to male students at an American university:

Our principal difficulty was ... a number of people who'd had affairs with girls or had had another interesting experience, and wanted to come in and tell about it, straight away. That is not a theme. A theme is something that is worth something to everybody.

(Frank O'Connor, interview with Anthony Whittier,
in *Writers at Work*, 1959)

Ideas into words

Moving from an idea to a fully-formed story is complex. Most writers use notebooks in which they collect observations to be used at a later date. A sound piece of advice that you will find in many handbooks on how to write short stories is: 'Don't be in too much of a rush to write the story itself.' Some claim that most of the work goes on before you write the story, and this is certainly reflected in William Boyd's comments below on 'Killing Lizards' (page 167). O'Connor's method started with four-line 'themes' containing essential characters, essential action but no details, his students often using algebraic symbols to outline the basic structure:

- X leaves home after an argument with Y.
- Y hears of X's death and remarries.
- X (not dead) writes letters to Y pretending to be tracing relatives.
- Y confesses failure of second marriage in letters.

Alternatively, some writers prefer to get on with the story as soon as possible. The French short story writer Guy de Maupassant (1850–1893) recommended 'getting black on white' so that you can 'see' the whole story and then go back and rework it.

Redrafting

Undoubtedly you have redrafted your own work and have perhaps found this the least rewarding part of writing. But for some writers this is the most important stage, and the most enjoyable:

> I like to mess around with my stories. I'd rather tinker with a story after writing it, and then tinker some more, changing this, changing that, than have to write the story in the first place. That initial writing just seems to me the hard place I have to get to in order to go on and have fun with the story. Rewriting for me is not a chore – it's something I like to do ... Maybe I revise because it gradually takes me into the heart of what the story is about. I have to keep trying to see if I can find that out. It's a process more than a fixed position.
>
> (Raymond Carver, *No Heroics Please*, 1991)

Going public

Stories may start off as the expression of personal feelings, but they very quickly become the property of publishers, editors, compilers, teachers. More than any other form of creative writing, short stories are institutionalised – that is, they are controlled by various authorities who take charge of the creative process. Initially, this is through magazines and journals – where most short stories are first published. This includes popular magazines such as *Woman's Own*, *Bella* or *Cosmopolitan*, as well as literary magazines. Some of these also run competitions for new writers and these are listed in annual guidebooks for writers and artists, which can usually be found in library reference sections.

Another route, and another institution, is the creative writing course. Particularly in the USA, these courses are now extremely popular (there are around one hundred to choose from) and there is usually some emphasis on short stories in spite of the relatively small market for this kind of writing. In the UK it was not possible to study the writing of short stories and poetry until the recent establishment of a novel writing course at Manchester University. Many of these courses have their own in-house journals in which the students' work is published.

Stories are less amenable to performance than poetry, and so readings by short story writers are almost unknown. In

Britain, the BBC broadcasts short stories every week-day and receives hundreds of scripts per month, often by new writers. So, in short, opportunities for encouraging the would-be writer are increasingly varied, but collections of short stories do not sell well and are not favoured by publishers.

Here are two examples of how stories in this collection were produced:

'The Yellow Wallpaper' by Charlotte Perkins Gilman

The circumstances in which 'The Yellow Wallpaper' was written are well documented. The story must be seen in the context of the treatment of mental disorder in women in the nineteenth century. It is also closely linked to the circumstances of Gilman's life. Suffering from depression shortly after her marriage in 1884, Gilman turned to the famous doctor, S. Weir Mitchell, for treatment. Mitchell's 'rest cure' treatment is described here by Elaine Showalter:

> The standard treatment for neuraesthenia (a nervous disorder) was Silas Weir Mitchell's rest cure, a technique that this distinguished American neurologist had developed after the Civil War. Mitchell's rest cure, which he first described in 1873, depended upon seclusion, massage, electricity, immobility, and diet. When his neuraesthenic subjects … became thin, tense, fretful and depressed, Mitchell ordered them to enter a clinic for 'a combination of entire rest and of excessive feeding made possible by passive exercise obtained through steady use of massage and electricity'. For six weeks the patient was isolated from her family and friends, confined to bed, forbidden to sit up, sew, read, write, or do any intellectual work, visited daily by the physician, and fed and massaged by the nurse. She was expected to gain as much as fifty pounds on a diet that began with milk and gradually built up to several substantial meals a day.
>
> (Elaine Showalter, *The Female Malady*, 1985, p. 138)

Gilman herself was given this treatment, but, she wrote in her own journal, *The Forerunner*, in 1913:

> I went home and obeyed those instructions for some three months, and came so near the borderline of utter mental ruin that I could see over.

Thus she wrote 'The Yellow Wallpaper' in reaction to those experiences:

> It was not intended to drive people crazy, but to save people from being crazy, and it worked.

'Killing Lizards' by William Boyd

Here William Boyd recalls the writing of this story after many years:

> 'Killing Lizards' was written in the second half of the seventies – 1977/78 if I recall. I was in my mid-twenties and was at Oxford doing a PhD in English Literature at the time. My literary efforts were concentrated largely on short stories (though I was also writing a novel as well as teaching, researching a thesis and writing book reviews) as it seemed to me that for an unpublished writer (as I then was) short stories had a better chance of seeing the light of day than novels.
>
> The story's background is very much my own. I was born in Ghana and brought up there and in Nigeria. The setting of the story, though it's not explicit, is the campus of the University of Ibadan, Nigeria, where my father was chief medical officer. Like the boys in the story, me and my friends (aged 12–14) used to roam the campus (which was vast) with our catapults killing lizards, or indeed letting fly at anything that moved, including snakes, squirrels, birds – but lizards were our main target, bloodthirsty little so-and-so's that we were.
>
> The incidents of the story, however, are entirely fictional and the character of Gavin is entirely remote from me, or, so I like to think, the type of person I was. However, I was using my African background a fair amount at the time, using it as the setting for a number of stories. I would write them in longhand

(in pencil) fairly quickly and then retype them. The editing process varied a great deal, but normally I never start to write until everything has been figured out, so that there is a period of 'invention' – note-making, narrative-outlining, character-naming etc – that can last any amount of time before the relatively fluent and rapid first draft.

(personal communication, 1996)

✦ *Activities*

1 Reread 'The Yellow Wallpaper' either individually or in a small group. Compare the treatment of the woman in the story with Showalter's account of Mitchell's 'rest cure'. Make a checklist of things that do and do not happen. How satisfying an explanation of the story do you find this? What else contributes to the woman's madness?

2 Reread William Boyd's account of his writing of 'Killing Lizards'. Imagine a similar account written by any other author in this collection to explain one of the stories. Using the biographical information on pages 156–161 and the additional information in this section, write such an account. You will need to use your imagination and you may wish to do some further research using a school or public library.

──────────── ✦ ────────────

What types of texts are these short stories?

Perhaps the first thing to remember is that a short story is not just a story that is short! Modern short stories usually have several features in common and, as you will see later in this section, many literary theorists have tried to define exactly what those features are. But individual stories also borrow from other forms of writing, making use of a variety of ways of telling stories.

Many of the activities that accompany these Resource Notes assume that you have already read several stories from this anthology.

♦ *Activity*

Working with someone else if possible, create a list of ways in which people produce stories or fiction in the real world, for example a newspaper story. Concentrate on short forms, leaving out novels. Put your list in rank order from those forms which are most like short stories to those which are least like short stories, giving your reasons. For example, jokes can be like short stories because they usually lead up to a point or a twist at the end so that the whole thing makes sense. Can you add to the list below?

- newspaper stories
- anecdotes (oral)
- letters
- advertising
- magazine articles
- reports
- minutes.

Borrowed forms

Short stories can in fact borrow from any of these forms and some recent experimental stories deliberately present a fragmented text consisting entirely of borrowed forms. For example, 'Computers Don't Argue' by Gordon R. Dickson (in *Short Story Workshop*, Cambridge University Press, 1990) consists entirely of letters.

There is no straightforward answer to the question of which form is most like the short story. Some writers claim that short stories share the purpose of short poems (lyrical poetry). Others prefer to emphasise the influence of journalism and oral stories. Obviously short stories have a number of common features, but there are many ways in which they can differ.

They usually concentrate on a crisis or a situation, revealing a character's or an observer's feelings about what has happened. There has been an increasing tendency in recent years to play down plot and to emphasise instead a feeling or situation to be revealed. Many readers feel disappointed because of this; they expect a strong plot with a 'twist in the tail', but are instead asked to search for significant patterns of meaning once they have finished the story. In this respect short stories have much in common with short poems and so they should perhaps be treated as poems, with close engagement given to the author's choice of words.

Frank O'Connor, an Irish short story writer (see also page 155), said that the short story usually looks at isolated individuals who undergo a frontier experience. Here, isolation can be physical, psychological or social, and a 'frontier experience' involves some kind of significant moment, like the experience of the death of a relative, that changes your perspective in some way. For example, Col, in 'The Badness Within Him', is isolated by his state of limbo between childhood and adulthood. His father's death is the crisis that moves Col some way forward through the frontier of his adolescence. A frontier in this sense can be anything from the borders of sanity to a point of change in a man's attitude towards women. A recent extension of the idea is that the short story has become increasingly pessimistic in its outlook, such that characters frequently come in sight of the frontier but fail to cross it. Which stories in this collection take this pessimistic view?

✦ *Activities*

1 Draw up a chart indicating which stories contain the features O'Connor mentions. Remember that the presence of these features does not necessarily make them useful in your reading. That is for you to decide.

2 What has the short story got in common with each of the forms below? To do this you will need to identify the essential features of each. Identify which stories in this collection share those features.

- poems
- sketches
- tales
- oral stories
- journalism
- essays
- films
- still photographs
- practice for writing a novel.

For example, journalism is associated with magazines and newspapers. It is writing that keeps up to date with world events; it is designed to be read once and is quickly discarded. Some short stories are like this, especially when they appear in magazines which are thrown away after a few months. Production time for a short story is considerably less than that required by a novel, but in what sense can these short stories be said to be up to date?

Critics' comments

✦ *Activity*

The following comments have been made by critics comparing short stories with the forms listed on page 171. Using the ideas presented in this section, choose the stories you think are most typical of each of the forms described below.

Sketches, essays and tales

Helmut Bonheim claims that a sketch (like a character portrait) essentially describes, an essay primarily comments or argues, and a tale reports or narrates events. A short story combines all three forms (*The Narrative Modes*, Brewer, 1982, p. 3).

Poems (1)

Bernard O'Donoghue draws links between the short story and the Shakespearian sonnet:

> We might note the formal parallel of the short poem, especially the Shakespearian sonnet (three quatrains and a couplet) with the tendency of the couplet to reverse the development of the first twelve lines.
>
> (*The English Review*, September 1992)

Poems (2)

The language of poetry is often analysed in great depth, but this is much less common with short stories. Dominic Head (*The Modernist Short Story*, Cambridge University Press, 1992) feels that complex symbolism is commonly detected in poetry, but is rarely observed in discussion of short fiction. Some of the symbols used in these short stories are:

- a red dress
- killing lizards
- terrible screaming
- a ghost

- a house
- a pair of glasses
- a car dump
- a manual of mechanics.

Journalism

The American writer Edgar Allan Poe is generally regarded as having defined the modern short story in 1842 (*Review of Hawthorne's 'Twice Told Tales'*, in *Graham's Magazine*). In this respect, Poe was ahead of his time because he anticipated the 'throwaway culture' of the twentieth century. He did this by promoting short stories published in magazines, claiming that part of their value came from their short-lived nature. Appearing in this form they also had the advantage of immediacy over the novel, which often took several years to produce. Thus, right from the moment of its definition, the short story has been linked with the commercial world.

Oral stories

Originally, stories were told face to face by one person to another or by one person to a group. They were made up spontaneously or were improvised around a basic framework. The modern short story has come a long way since then, but sometimes writers like to retain some of these earlier features. For example, the use of repetition and a 'frame narrator' who appears at the beginning and end of the story.

Films and photographs

Valerie Shaw writes that:

> … it has become virtually a commonplace to point out that photography in the form of cinema is closely allied to the short story.
>
> (*The Short Story*, Longman, 1983, p. 14)

In films, there is rarely someone explaining the significance of what happens – we have to work it out for ourselves. Perhaps an even better analogy is that of a 'snapshot' where the aim of both photographer and writer is to capture the significance of one particular moment, leaving out everything else that happened. You might consider the usefulness of films and photographs to explain what short stories achieve.

Practice for writing a novel

Could Jane Austen's novel *Pride and Prejudice* or T. S. Eliot's poem *The Wasteland* have been written as homework? According to Andrew Levy:

> The short story continues to be treated as the genre for apprenticeship.
>
> (*The Culture and Commerce of the American Short Story*,
> Cambridge University Press, 1993, p. 105)

In other words, people often see short stories as the kind of writing you do when you are learning your trade, but not when you become a fully-fledged writer. Arguably this is why short stories have less status than novels: the immense popularity of writing courses in America has reinforced this view as well as made the USA the country of the modern short story. Many great writers, such as James Joyce and William Faulkner, wrote short stories in their earlier years but then progressed to novels.

◆

How do these short stories present their subjects?

A short story is the result of many choices made by the writer, so that the style of the finished text is a pattern of symbols, themes, characters, plot and, of course, language. This section suggests a variety of activities for exploring some aspects of the presentation of these stories. You may find that further ideas are triggered off by them.

✦ *Activities*

'The July Ghost'

1 Diagrammatic representation of a story can often help to clarify its themes. Try to represent the situation in 'The July Ghost' as a diagram. Include the following elements:
   - the man
   - the woman
   - the barrier between them
   - the ghost
   - the real boy
   - the feelings of the characters
   - any others that you think are important.

   If you feel that changes take place during the story you may wish to show the passing of time. Or you could draw two diagrams. Compare your diagram with somebody else's, find evidence to support your diagram in the text and then create a new diagram on the basis of this discussion.

2 A symbol in a story is usually an image that stands for something else, often an underlying abstract idea. Here, A. S. Byatt has taken the ghost story form but is also using it to approach a more sensitive theme.

a Make two columns, one for the man, the other for the woman, and compare them with regard to the following:

- the ghost
- illusions
- talk
- action
- occupation
- the house/the garden
- sex
- any other features of the story you see as relevant.

b Working with a partner, prepare two brief preliminary reports that begin: 'The man's problem is …' and 'The woman's problem is …'. Include recommendations for how each needs to change, if at all.

'Red Dress – 1946'

A theme of this story is the main character's first steps towards adulthood. Explore this idea by doing the following:

1 The girl never tells her mother how she feels about her. Imagine that just before the dance a row develops. In pairs improvise this scene.

2 Throughout the story there are four influences on the girl's behaviour: boys, her friend Lonnie, Mary Fortune, and her mother. In a group of five, decide what kind of influence each of these people has. Work out a role play in which one of you takes the part of the girl. Improvise the workings of her mind when each of these people tries to influence her. Each character could address her in turn and she could answer them. How does she resist their point of view? Where does this leave her?

'The Day of the Butterfly'

1 Myra is the outsider in this story. Discuss any similar outsiders that you have experienced (some tact may be called for here). Make a list of the kind of people who could in any sense be considered outsiders, for example the homeless.

Consider if they are outsiders and what it is that makes others treat them as such, especially young children. Does this discussion raise any possible themes for this story?

2 The last scene of this story, when Myra is alone with Helen, is particularly dense in its imagery and ideas. Using a computer, rearrange some of the words in this section, adding a few of your own if you wish, to make a poem expressing how Helen feels at that moment. Experiment with different combinations of words in different spatial arrangements. Think of an appropriate title.

'Killing Lizards'

1 The relationships in this story can be approached through the symbolism of the Ancient Greek myth of Oedipus:

> Queen Jocasta and King Laius of Thebes are told by a prophet that their son Oedipus will murder his father and marry his mother. Wishing to avoid this calamity they leave their son on a mountainside to die, but he is found by a shepherd and brought up as the son of another king and queen. However, on growing up, Oedipus hears the same warning his parents had heard, and so leaves home. On the road he meets a stranger, argues with him and kills him. When he arrives at Thebes he successfully answers the riddle of the sphinx, is made King and marries the newly widowed queen. When Oedipus discovers that he has killed his father and married his mother, he blinds himself and Jocasta kills herself.

The psychoanalyst Sigmund Freud used this story to explain an aspect of boys' growing up. For Freud it is normal for boys to experience unconscious conflict with their father over their love for their mother. The conflict is resolved when boys identify with their father and realise that they must seek a partner of their own. In short, Freud saw this as an important part of the way in which boys grow up and become independent of their mothers. Do you find this idea a good explanation of what happens in this story? Find details in the story that either fit this explanation or seem to require some adjustment of it. For example, what is Gavin's relationship with his father? What is the evidence that Gavin is growing up? Discuss the following:

- Gavin's feelings towards his mother early in the story;
- your reaction to the killing of the lizards and how the text wants you to react;
- Gavin's feelings at the end of the story. For Freud the blinding of Oedipus is symbolic of what people feel (they don't want to 'see' the facts) when something shocking is revealed to them. Look for references to 'vision' after Gavin discovers his mother. Consider the adequacy of Freud's explanation.

2 Compare this story with 'The Badness Within Him'. Consider the common elements:

- a teenage boy
- his relationship with his family
- his experience of a traumatic event
- changes after that event.

To what extent do these stories present males growing up in a similar way?

'Dragons' Breath'

1 The story plays with the idea that myth is constantly being re-made. For example, one prominent myth in modern society is of the creation of a monster that we can't control. This story surfaced in the form of *Frankenstein* (Mary Shelley, 1818) in the last century and, arguably, has re-emerged in such films as *Robocop* (1987). How many modern examples of the following myths can you think of?

- conquering the unknown
- disruption of the family
- children know best

- animals have personalities
- true love
- wild children
- evil women.

2a In a small group, produce a series of news items to capture every angle of this story. You may like to use newspaper articles, radio and TV news flashes, bulletins and interviews with those involved, etc. Try to cover the villagers' lives before and after what happened, their feelings towards it, their personal losses, and the events themselves.

b Write a log/commentary on the production of your news coverage. Include:

- your choice of subject matter for each kind of news item;
- what you left out;
- which aspects of the story were easy or difficult to deal with;
- the differences between your news items and the style of the original story.

Consider:

- how characters were referred to;
- beginnings and endings;
- how the setting was described;
- the role of the narrator as a commentator;
- the use of direct speech;
- the use of repetition, etc.

'The Badness Within Him'

1 Converting a text into another form is a useful way of revealing its style. In pairs or on your own, choose a short passage from this story – not more than about one page in length.

a Produce the first draft of a storyboard for the extract and a commentary explaining your decisions, for example why you may have deliberately left something out or how you dealt with Col's thoughts or changes in point of view.

b Photocopy the extract and make a display comparing the two forms, and commenting on any intended effects on the reader/viewer.

2 This story explores the powerful and confused emotions of a young teenage boy. Make notes on the following elements in your reading of this story:

* the ways in which Col is isolated from his family (Does he want this or not?);
* the significance of the weather;
* Col's desire for change;
* things being the same;
* the power of Col's fear and anger;
* Col's childhood memories.

'The Yellow Wallpaper'

1 The presentation of madness in this story depends a great deal on the differing views of the characters. Make a list of the narrator's beliefs about her condition and map these against John's opinions as the story progresses. For example:

John's view	The narrator's view	Comment
'He does not believe I am sick!' (p. 81)	'John is a physician, and *perhaps* ... *perhaps* that is one reason I do not get well faster.' (p. 81)	She has some insight but she is very tentative.

Leave two blank columns and add comments to your chart addressing the following:

* how her attitude and feelings towards John change as the story progresses;
* how the descriptions of the wallpaper change as the story progresses.

2 Construct a graph comparing (a) the narrator's 'mad behaviour' with (b) her insight into her own situation and its causes. Plot two separate lines, one for (a) and one for (b). Label your axes as below using page numbers and selected moments for the horizontal axis:

Time

Use the graph to discuss the relationship between the main character's madness and her insight into her situation and its causes.

'Thief'

Why is the man's wallet returned with nothing stolen? This story is probably one of the most straightforward in this collection. It can be read as a cautionary tale – a warning to those who indulge in certain kinds of behaviour. It also has one of the strongest and most tightly constructed plots.

1 Reread the story and trace its plot elements in the following terms:
- what the reader knows on first reading;
- what the man knows or thinks;
- what the woman knows;
- what the police think.

For example, at the beginning of the story, the reader probably thinks the man is the thief and the woman is the victim.

Construct a table with four columns and chart the major developments through the story. Share your chart with someone else and discuss any points of disagreement. Why is the story written in this way?

2 Use this framework as the basis for a story of your own that involves a 'twist in the tail'. You could begin with a main character who has certain intentions or purposes that fail. If possible, make your ending one where the character is somehow punished for this behaviour.

'A Rose for Emily'

1 Most of the events in the story are very carefully dated, but the story is not told in chronological order. The list below gives most of the main events in their chronological order. Reread the story, noting down the order in which these events are actually told or mentioned in the story. With a partner, carefully compare the chronological order with the order of narrating – you may wish to construct a timeline to show this. Suggest reasons why Faulkner chose this order. Consider the effect on the reader; the creation of suspense or curiosity; and the creation of Emily's character. If you have responded to this story in slow motion (see page 192), use those responses to discuss how the order of events affected you.

- 1894 – the remission of Emily's taxes;
- the death of Emily's father;
- the arrival and courting of Homer Barron;
- buying the poison;
- Homer Barron deserts Emily;
- the smell;
- Emily's door remains closed;
- Emily gives china-painting lessons;
- the Board of Aldermen visit Emily;
- Emily's death;
- Emily's funeral;
- breaking into the room.

2 Is it possible to construct a gendered reading of this story? Charlotte Perkins Gilman and Janet Frame present women who retreat into 'madness' in their stories, which are linked with their own lives. It is usually women who do not fit into some man-made mould and with no other means of escape who suffer this fate.

Explore the idea that Emily Grierson is the victim of gender oppression in 'A Rose for Emily'. You might like to consider gender in relation to the following:

- the original authority for the tax remission;
- Emily's status;
- the town's authorities;
- ways in which Emily flouts convention;
- Emily's attitude towards her potential suitors;
- the officials' public and private attitude to Emily;
- the house itself;
- the town's attitude to marriage;
- Homer Barron's attitude to marriage;
- forcing into the room at the end (this also happens in 'The Yellow Wallpaper').

'Diary of a Madman'

1a In pairs, decide which incidents or moments in the story plot the progress of the man's madness. What is it about each incident that makes the man mad? Divide a page into two columns. Put the incidents/moments on one side, indicating what the problem is on the right hand side. For example:

Incident / moment	Problem
Imagining that the two dogs are talking, but nevertheless thinking that he must be drunk (p. 59)	He is suffering from delusions though he is still rational to some extent.

b Plot a graph using the above points. For the vertical axis use the man's degree of madness. Use the diary dates for the horizontal axis. Compare your graph with someone else's and discuss any points of disagreement.

2 The theme of a story can sometimes be revealed in the way that a character talks about others. In pairs, make a list of all the ways in which the main character refers to people throughout the story. Include plurals, titles and categories of people. What can you suggest about the causes of the man's state of mind, given the ways that he thinks about those around him?

'The Terrible Screaming'

Reread the story, but stop reading just before the fourth paragraph from the end. Rewrite the ending to make it predictable, conventional and satisfying. Think about:

- what happens to the Distinguished Stranger;
- the answers to the Specialist's questions;
- what happens to the screaming.

What do you find unusual about the style of this story? Consider the characters, the setting and the structure.

'Dossy'

On second reading, you may see this story in a very different light. Reread the story and look closely at:

- the details of the 'conversation' between Dossy and the little girl;
- what the little girl thinks of Dossy;
- the words used to describe Dossy and her possessions.

How do these images help to reveal the main theme of this story?

'The Waste Land' and 'Popular Mechanics'

Typical short story style is often revealed in the first few lines. The following exercise may help to indicate this. In a famous piece of research a boy was asked to describe a set of pictures in front of him. Read the boy's description below, and work out what must have been in the pictures. What makes this passage difficult to understand? Decide which words contribute to those difficulties. What assumptions is the boy making about his audience?

> They're playing football and he kicks it and it goes through there it breaks the window and they're looking at it and he comes out and shouts at them because they've broken it so they run away and then she looks out and she tells them off.
> (Basil Bernstein, *Class, Codes and Control*, Vol 2, Routledge & Kegan Paul, 1972)

1 Now reread the openings of 'The Waste Land' and 'Popular Mechanics' (from line 6). Compare the style of these two stories with the above passage. What assumptions do they make and what effect does this have on you when you first read these stories?

2 Twentieth-century short stories have frequently used pronouns ('she', 'we', 'they', etc) at the beginning before the name of the character is given. It is much more common in other kinds of speech and writing to use a name first and then a pronoun once the audience knows who you are talking about. When this is reversed, as in these short stories, it is known as cataphoric reference.

Compare the beginnings of the other stories in this collection. How many of them use cataphoric reference? Which types of stories tend to use this method? How do they continue in the presentation of the characters?

Moments of Madness – paired readings

Below is a list of themes and approaches covered by the stories in this collection:

- growing up
- parent–child relationships
- the class system/social structure
- gender roles
- conformity
- the causes of madness
- allegory
- relationships
- outsiders
- objective narration
- cataphoric reference.

For example, the presentation of madness can be considered by comparing 'Diary of a Madman' and 'The Yellow Wallpaper'. You might like to think about the following:

- point of view: the kind of language used to convey the characters' thoughts and feelings;
- the progress of madness: the events that trigger off the crisis and the kinds of feelings presented;
- the context of each story: that is, the part played by the setting or social context of the story;
- how the two stories reach a climax;
- where your sympathies lie and how the story attempts to manipulate the reader's feelings towards the characters;
- what causes of madness are implied by the stories.

Here are some suggested pairings of the stories (pairings suggested elsewhere and stories by the same author have been left out):

- 'Dragons' Breath' and 'The Terrible Screaming'
- 'The Yellow Wallpaper' and 'A Rose for Emily'
- 'Thief' and 'Red Dress'
- 'The Day of the Butterfly' and 'Diary of a Madman'
- 'Dossy' and 'Day of the Butterfly'.

✦ *Activity*

In pairs or small groups, decide on which themes can be explored with which pairings. Add your own ideas to both lists if possible.

───────────────────── ✦ ─────────────────────

Who reads these short stories and how do they interpret them?

The process of reading

In the past, many critics have forgotten that it takes time to read a story and that, as a result, your interpretation unfolds slowly, often in highly individual ways. So it is important not only to consider what kinds of text you have in front of you, but also what happens when you read and what kind of reader you are.

Below are two readers' first reactions to 'The Badness Within Him'. They are notes jotted down as the students read the story.

✦ *Activities*

1 Analyse these students' responses. What kinds of things are they concerned about as they read? With a partner, categorise these responses in a similar way to the examples given below.

Charlie's responses:

These were made in writing as he read the story. The first three responses are explained:

- Night before what? – Here he is attempting to make predictions.
- Religious – perhaps not? – Trying to work out a theme for the story.
- Why is he bad? – Trying to understand the characters.
- Why doesn't he like the sun?
- 'They' – the family?
- Were they staying all August? Perhaps he burns easily? (sunburn on Jess).
- Perhaps his badness prevents him from liking the sun?
- Character is called Col (short for Colin).

- Quite young, not a teenager.
- Unpleasant comment – resents Jess growing up.
- He hates it there.
- Emotion – frightened? Emotionless character?
- Doesn't like stagnation – gets bored.
- Set in seaside town possibly not English – it was always sunny.
- Dog on his shoulder – is this the same as a chip?
- Yet to say anything pleasant.
- Mother seems to be tried continually by Col.
- 'Sea creatures, West Cliff' – suggests English place.
- London – confirms England.

(responses up to page 11)

2a Now read Louise's responses to the same story. Categorise her responses and prepare to talk for two minutes about how she reads this story differently from Charlie.

Louise's responses

These were made after having been told that it is the first chapter of a novel.

- What on earth is he on about? – the badness within him?
- Is this religious? Catholic?
- Night before what?
- This boy is restless, bored. He's young, thoughtful.
- Doesn't *sound* like a child.
- Boy's name is Col – makes the story sound old. 1950s.
- Sounds like one of those tacky stories of 'lost childhoods'.
- What is a black dog and what is it doing on his shoulder?
- This is odd. It doesn't flow. It jumps around.
- Why does this boy think he's evil/bad? The deeper ideas are getting lost in the very dull story.
- The idea of this desolate/lonely child doesn't gel with 'the badness within him'.

- His father's drowned. So what? I really don't care about the characters.
- Last two and a half sides are a let down. They don't fit in with the oppressed tone of the rest of the book.

2b For both Charlie and Louise, write a short paragraph which describes the 'reading' each has made of the story. For example, you might say of Louise, 'She is far more evaluative than Charlie. At an early stage she makes strong judgements of the characters, the events and the whole story …'. Alternatively, you may wish to analyse someone else's reading of this story.

3 If you have not already done so, create your own first reading of 'The Badness Within Him', using a similar technique to the one shown above. Try the same technique on any of the stories in this collection. Keep these ideas for further development in the activities in the other sections of the resource notes.

Reading short stories/reading novels

It is suggested in the Introduction to this book that novels and short stories (and poems) are not read in the same way. In the activity on page 7, a group of students were told that 'The Badness Within Him' is the first chapter of a novel. They were then asked for their reactions when told that it is in fact a complete short story. Below is a selection from their written responses.

✦ *Activities*

1 What are your own reactions? Which of the responses below do you agree/disagree with? Are there others that you would like to add?

- 'No plot. Boy is angry, father dies, boy feels guilty. Not really a very good storyline.'
- 'It would make you think about it more though.'

- 'Pointless – as short story too many questions left unanswered.'
- 'The characters are not detailed. They would appear primarily as needless fillers.'
- 'More sorrow towards Col is created. Because it ends so soon, could feel sorry for boy feeling this way. (If it were longer, illusion is he has time to make peace with himself.)'
- 'It would make you think about it more/deeper.'
- 'By itself it's more enjoyable/thought provoking than as part of a novel. No plot but it's better.'
- 'I think it would have a completely different meaning to me, i.e. I would feel it had to be symbolising something else, i.e. have a message to it.'
- 'The death of the father would be in the right place as before (if it were the first chapter of a novel) it came too early.'

2 The following general points can be made about reading short stories. They are intended as useful guidelines rather than rigid rules about the way that short stories are read:

- A short story is usually read more symbolically than a novel. For example, the setting cannot be so concerned with detailed re-creation of a place. Setting must be seen as significant to some central 'point'.
- When reading short stories there is more of a tendency to generalise – 'to see eternity in a grain of sand' – otherwise the details presented would appear too sketchy to be satisfying (E. Hutchens, in M. Spilka (ed.), *Towards a Poetics of Fiction*, 1979, p. 59).
- Characterisation tends to be symbolic rather than naturalistic. Characters are much less fully developed than in novels.
- There is far more to remember in a novel and so the reader divides it up into larger 'chunks' in memory – whole scenes or episodes tend to be the units in which novels are

discussed. Short stories require closer attention to the words.

- The reader's knowledge of the length of a story creates expectations and so affects the interpretation of particular details. Think about how differently you would watch a film if you were told it was 10 minutes long rather than 90.
- Short stories work more by implication than direct statement.
- In short stories there is often a conflict between plots and patterns. Readers gain their first satisfaction from the movement of the plot, but often more complete enjoyment comes when at the end you look back to uncover the patterns in the text. You read plots forward and meaning backwards; that is, you cannot fully understand the whole pattern until you get to the end. 'Pattern' refers to recurring images, significant moments and contrasts, the organisation of time and point of view, etc. In many short stories the plot is kept to a minimum and so a quick read can often lead to dissatisfaction.

Working with a partner, look back at the stories you have read. Drawing on a range of stories, find examples of as many of the above points as you can.

Reading in slow motion

Another good way of looking at your own process of reading a short story is to take the simplest and one of the shortest stories in this collection – 'Thief' – and stop to record your responses at various stages of your reading. Suggested stopping points are:

- at the end of the first paragraph;
- at the end of the first page;
- at the end of the second page;
- before the final paragraph;
- at the end.

This can lead to what might be called a micro reading – an intensely detailed reading of the text, almost like reading in slow motion.

✦ Activities

1 Before reading the following responses, read the first paragraph of 'Thief', covering up the rest of the story with a piece of paper, and then respond in writing.

Here are several readers' responses to the first paragraph:

- **Guy:** The man obviously fancies the woman. Could he become one of these fatal attraction people?
- **Siobhan:** Is she trying to hide or is she embarrassed that the man is watching her? Love story – man looking for lost love.
- **Helen:** Man travelling, every day, ordinary man – nothing special. Woman – rich, business-like (bun, purse) – stuck up, knows she has good looks.
- **Ralf:** 'He' could be the thief. Or could be 'thief' as in the stealing of a heart, as in a love story, in which case the woman may be the thief.
- **Kevin:** You don't think about the setting as the description is all about the woman and the man's actions.

These brief extracts show the immense variety possible even with such a straightforward text. For example, the above readers do the following: they bring ideas to the text (you might say that the text reads them – by bringing stereotypical ideas out of them) including stereotypes about the behaviour of men and women (Ralf), and they go beyond the information given in the text, making assumptions about the characters' thoughts and feelings (Helen).

2 What else do these readers do with the text? Compare this with your own responses to the first paragraph. Then continue to respond at the recommended points. Aim to

expand your response repertoire using the possibilities raised above.

Dimensions of reading

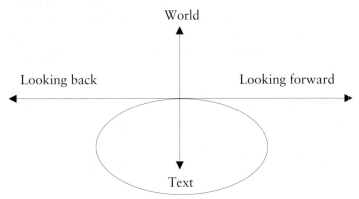

On first reading, you read, in a sense, in four dimensions. You look inwards at the text, focussing carefully on the words on the page; you look outwards at the world in which you live and gather ideas from it; you look backwards at what you have previously read, recalling details and general impressions; you look forwards at text to come, predicting the general shape of the story ('love story?'), the identity of the characters, and what will happen next. Which of these did you do most often?

✦ Activities

1 Reread 'Thief' and respond without looking at your responses to your first reading. Use your second response and the above model to think about what happens on second reading. In a sense a fifth dimension is opened up because you now know the whole text as you read. What happens? How is your second reading altered by this fifth dimension? How is your slowed-down reading of 'Thief' affected by knowing the whole story?

2 Imagine that you will be entirely alone for several years and that the only non-essential item you are allowed is two short stories from this collection. Make your choice, bearing in mind that, as you will read your selected stories several times, the fifth dimension is likely to be an important factor in your decision. Discuss with a partner which stories best stand up to repeated readings and then write an essay justifying your selection. You may wish to consider the following:

- how the plot is affected
- characterisation
- the whole pattern of themes and images
- the writer's use of repetition and variation
- the impact of the beginning and the ending.

◆

GLOSSARY

'The Badness Within Him'

10   **chintz curtains:** curtains made of material printed with flowers and other patterns

11   **scullery:** a small room attached to a kitchen for washing dishes, etc.

12   **bladder-wrack:** a type of seaweed

13   **crenellated:** with battlements

16   **the cenotaph:** a monument in Whitehall, London, commemorating the dead of two world wars

17   **sepia photographs:** an early form of photograph with a characteristic brown hue

'Day of the Butterfly'

19   **Grade One, Grade Six:** roughly the equivalent of the bottom and top year groups in a British primary school
        solicitude: anxiety, concern

25   **taffeta:** a plain woven, glossy material, often silk

29   **ether:** a chemical used as an anaesthetic

'Red Dress – 1946'

31   **treadle machine:** an old-fashioned sewing machine, worked by means of a foot pedal
        basting: tacking, a temporary fixing of the cloth before it is sewn permanently
        organdie: a thin, stiff, translucent cotton
        a poke bonnet: a bonnet with a projecting rim worn in the early nineteenth century
        tam: a cloth cap

32   **a Blue Baby:** a baby suffering from a disease caused by lack of oxygenated blood

33   **cashmere wool:** soft wool from Kashmiri goats
        mother of pearl: the decorative pattern on the inside of shells such as oysters and mussels

34	**burlesqued:** imitating, mocking
35	**flannelette:** imitation flannel

The Last Days of Pompeii: Pompeii was an ancient town in Italy that was buried by the lava from an erupting volcano in AD79.

Xs and Os: noughts and crosses

36 **peplum:** a short ornamental strip hanging from the waistline of a skirt

bobby-pin: a type of hair pin

37 **fluted paper:** paper folded into grooves

44 **Paisley kimono:** a Japanese style gown with a pear-shaped design

'Killing Lizards'

45 **bole:** the trunk of a tree

48 **coruscating:** sparkling

49 **ammoniacal:** like ammonia, strong smelling

phials: small glass containers

51 **Jungle-Jim:** usually spelt 'gym' – a climbing frame

'Diary of a Madman'

57 **Director:** This and many of the titles in this story require some knowledge of the Russian civil service of the time. Today, a civil servant is a government employee who usually carries out administrative tasks. In nineteenth-century Russia, the civil service included doctors and university professors as well as the military and the courts. Although not in the table opposite, the Director is referred to as 'His Excellency' and this gives an indication of his rank.

His Excellency: See note to page 57 above.

kopeck: one hundredth of a rouble (see below)

58 **drozhky:** a low four-wheeled open carriage

rouble: the main Russian monetary unit

petitioner: someone who makes a formal request to the Government

Civilian ranks in the Russian Civil Service, 1722–1917		
Class	*Civilian rank*	*Form of address*
1	Chancellor	Your Supreme Excellency
2	Actual Privy Councillor	Your Supreme Excellency
3	Privy Councillor	Your Excellency
4	Actual State Councillor	Your Excellency
5	State Councillor	Your Excellency
6	Collegiate Councillor	Your Supreme Honour
7	Court Councillor	Your Supreme Honour
8	Collegiate Assessor	Your Supreme Honour
9	Titular Councillor	Your Honour
10	Collegiate Secretary	Your Honour
11	Ship's Secretary	Your Honour
12	Provincial Secretary (i)	Your Honour
13	Provincial Secretary (ii)	Your Honour
14	Collegiate Registrar	Your Honour

58 **Principals:** high ranking officials
    civil servants: See note to page 57 above.

60 **the Little Bee:** This is a reference to the Petersburg journal,
    The Northern Bee, which attacked writers such as Gogol and
    had police protection.

61 **Kursk:** a common name for a Russian town
    ambergris: a substance found in the intestine of a sperm
    whale and used to make perfume

62 **Pushkin:** Alexsandr Pushkin, influential romantic Russian
    poet (1799–1837)
    General: 'General' and 'director' are used interchangeably in
    this translation. 'General' was the equivalent military rank to
    'director'.

62   **pomade:** a scented ointment for the hair and scalp

63   **Ruch:** a famous tailor of the day
       the Russian fool, Filatka: the heroine of a play, *Four Bridegrooms and One Bride*, a comic portrayal of the life of a common man
       Collegiate Registrar: See table on page 199.

66   **plebeian:** common or coarse
       ye: the letter 'e' in the Russian alphabet

70   **jabot:** a frill on the front of a man's shirt

71   **titular councillor:** This was a lowish grade (ninth out of fourteen) but was by common consent the most comic grade of all. Ronald Hingley writes: 'The mere mention of a titular councillor was enough to create pleasurable tension in the reader, who could assume that some kind of slapstick comedy was likely to follow' (*Russian Writers and Society*, 1977).

72   **a mason:** a freemason, a member of the secret brotherhood of masons
       civil commotion: This refers to a dispute over the successor to Ferdinand VII, who died in 1833.
       donna: a lady

74   **Capuchin friar:** a kind of Franciscan monk. This is a jibe at King Philip II of Spain (1527–1598), who was a religious ally of the Capuchin monks.

75   **lorgnette:** opera glasses
       Judases: In the New Testament, Judas Iscariot was the apostle who betrayed Jesus.
       Mahommedanism: Islam

77   **Only chemists write letters:** Beatrice Scott's translation of this reads: 'Chemists write letters, first wetting their tongues with vinegar – otherwise their faces would be covered with tetter (a skin disease)' (*Stories from St Petersburg*, 1945).
       grandees: Spanish noblemen of high rank

78   **cooper:** a maker of casks and barrels

79   **the Inquisition:** the Roman Catholic Church's organisation for trying and punishing religious opponents. The Spanish Inquisition, which was notorious, was abolished in the nineteenth century.

       the Grand Inquisitor: leader of the Inquisition

       Polignac: Polignac was a foreign minister under King Charles X (1757–1836) of France.

80   **troika:** a cart drawn by three horses

       Dhey of Algiers: This is a reference to Hussein Pasha, who was deposed by the French in 1830.

'The Yellow Wallpaper'

81   **felicity:** happiness

82   **box:** an evergreen shrub

85   **wharf:** a bay for loading and unloading ships

87   **the Fourth of July:** American Independence Day

       Weir Mitchell: See page 166.

88   **debased Romanesque:** a poor imitation of the Romanesque style of architecture (c.10–12th centuries)

       delirium tremens: a form of delirium suffered by heavy drinkers

       fatuity: purposelessness

       a frieze: a horizontal strip of decorated wallpaper just below a ceiling

92   **arabesque:** a fancifully decorative style of architecture, originally Arabic

94   **mopboard:** skirting board

99   **plantain:** a tropical plant similar to a banana tree

'A Rose for Emily'

103   **cupolas:** domes

       scrolled: architecturally designed to imitate scrolled parchment

       cotton gins: machines for separating cotton from its seed

       august: respected

103 **Union and Confederate soldiers:** the two sides in the American Civil War (1861–1865)
the battle of Jefferson: a reference to the American Civil War, but the battle itself was invented by Faulkner
into perpetuity: indefinitely

104 **calligraphy:** the art of beautiful writing
the Board of Aldermen: local councillors

105 **temerity:** rashness, foolhardiness

106 **locusts:** locust trees, native to North America

107 **spraddled:** sprawling
a penny more or less: every penny would now make a difference

108 **Yankee:** someone from the north of the United States. During the American Civil War the northern states were opposed to slavery.
livery stable: a stable for horses
noblesse oblige: high rank carries with it certain obligations
craned: stretched
jalousies: window blinds
imperviousness: stubbornness,

110 **Episcopal:** a branch of the Anglican Church
cabal: plan, conspiracy

112 **sibilant:** hissing
bier: a carriage for transporting a coffin

113 **acrid pall:** bitter smell
valance: a curtain around a bed
cuckolded: been unfaithful to (a husband)

'Thief'

117 **Ebony-Tressed:** black haired

118 **Sak's and Peck & Peck and Lord & Taylor:** quality American department stores

'The July Ghost'

120 **faux pas:** blunder
vituperation: hatred

121 **mortice-locked:** dead-locked with a key

123 **Hardy:** Thomas Hardy, English novelist and poet (1840–1928)

124 **Kingsley Amis:** English twentieth-century novelist and academic (1922–1996)
Plath: Sylvia Plath (1932–1963), an American poet who committed suicide
Milletts: a British high street shop specialising in outdoor wear

127 **voluble:** talkative

129 **Hardy's original air-blue gown:** This is a line from Thomas Hardy's poem 'The Voice'. The reference is to clothing worn by Hardy's wife, whose death the poem laments.

130 **bowdlerize:** to censor; named after Thomas Bowdler (1754–1825), whose nineteenth-century editions of Shakespeare were abridged for a 'family' audience.
folie à deux: literally 'double madness', two people sharing the same delusions

134 **effigy:** image
rigor mortis: the stiffening of the body after death

'Dragons' Breath'

145 **primeval:** ancient

146 **sagacious:** shrewd, intelligent
truffles: edible fungus
ceps: edible mushrooms
vermilion: scarlet, dark red

148 **tump:** a small hill
whorls: patterns suggesting a whirling movement

150 **ennui:** boredom
noisome: harmful, objectionable

154 **paradisal light:** light of paradise

Resource Notes

159   **Mike Tyson:** (1966–) American heavyweight boxer of notorious power

      the American South: Faulkner was one of the authors most responsible for creating images of the American South – the lost cause, the rich land owner, the golden age before the war, the cavalier and the lady. In the nineteenth century, the South had been made prosperous by its warm climate, its vast plantations of cotton, sugar and tobacco, and its exploitation of slaves. The plantation owners became the equivalent of the lords of the manor in England, but it was as if slavery had put a curse on the land and this eventually led to the American Civil War in the 1860s. The South broke away from the other States, forming the Confederacy in order to uphold their right to continue with slavery. They lost the war and thus lost everything that had been part of their former glory.

160   **apartheid:** the political system of South Africa from 1948 until 1993, which segregated black and white people in every sphere of life

163   **putto:** Italian for male child; usually shown naked in Renaissance paintings

FURTHER READING

Susan Hill
The Albatross (Penguin, 1974)

I'm the King of the Castle (Penguin, 1974)

A Bit of Singing and Dancing (Penguin, 1975)

Mrs de Winter (Mandarin, 1994: a sequel to Daphne du Maurier's *Rebecca*)

Raymond Carver
The Stories of Raymond Carver (Pan, 1985)

Fires (Collins Harvill, 1994)

Charlotte Perkins Gilman
Herland (The Women's Press, 1979)

The Charlotte Perkins Gilman Reader (The Women's Press, 1981)

Alice Munro
Lives of Girls and Women (Penguin, 1982)

Dance of the Happy Shades (Penguin, 1983)

Friend of My Youth (Vintage, 1991)

Open Secrets (Vintage, 1994)

William Boyd
On the Yankee Station (Penguin, 1982)

The Blue Afternoon (Penguin, 1994)

The Destiny of Natalie X (Penguin, 1996)

Robley Wilson Jnr
Dancing for Men (University of Pittsburgh Press, 1983)

Terrible Kisses (Simon and Schuster, 1989)

The Victim's Daughter (Simon and Schuster, 1991)

A. S. Byatt

Sugar and Other Stories (Penguin, 1988)

Possession (Vintage, 1991)

The Matisse Stories (Vintage, 1994)

The Djinn in the Nightingale's Eye (Vintage, 1995)

Nikolai Gogol

Diary of a Madman and Other Stories (Penguin, 1972)

Plays and Petersburg Tales (Oxford University Press, 1995)

Janet Frame

You Are Now Entering the Human Heart (The Women's Press, 1984)

To the Island, An Angel at My Table, An Envoy from Mirror City (The Women's Press 1984; Frame's three-part autobiography)

The Lagoon and Other Stories (Bloomsbury, 1991)

Alan Paton

Cry the Beloved Country (Penguin, 1958)

Debbie Go Home (Penguin, 1965)

William Faulkner

The Sound and the Fury (Pan, 1989)

Collected Stories (Vintage, 1995)

As I Lay Dying (Vintage 1996)

CAMBRIDGE LITERATURE

◆

Ben Jonson *The Alchemist*

William Wycherley *The Country Wife*

Robert Burns *Selected Poems*

William Blake *Selected Works*

Jane Austen *Pride and Prejudice*

Jane Austen *Emma*

Mary Shelley *Frankenstein*

Three Victorian Poets

Charlotte Brontë *Jane Eyre*

Emily Brontë *Wuthering Heights*

Nathaniel Hawthorne *The Scarlet Letter*

Charles Dickens *Hard Times*

Charles Dickens *Great Expectations*

George Eliot *Silas Marner*

Thomas Hardy *Far from the Madding Crowd*

Henrik Ibsen *A Doll's House*

Robert Louis Stevenson *Treasure Island*

Mark Twain *Huckleberry Finn*

Thomas Hardy *Tess of the d'Urbervilles*

Oscar Wilde *The Importance of Being Earnest*

Kate Chopin *The Awakening and other stories*

Anton Chekhov *The Cherry Orchard*

James Joyce *Dubliners*

Six Poets of the Great War

D. H. Lawrence *Selected Short Stories*

Edith Wharton *The Age of Innocence*

F. Scott Fitzgerald *The Great Gatsby*

Virginia Woolf *A Room of One's Own*

Robert Cormier *After the First Death*

Caryl Churchill *The After-Dinner Joke*
and *Three More Sleepless Nights*

Graham Swift *Learning to Swim*

Fay Weldon *Letters to Alice*

Louise Lawrence *Children of the Dust*

Julian Barnes *A History of the World in 10½ Chapters*

Amy Tan *The Joy Luck Club*

Four Women Poets

Moments of Madness – 150 years of short stories

Helen Edmundson *The Mill on the Floss*